Chapter 1

MY EYES STRAYED TO those of Detective Inspector Jennifer Griffiths. I looked away almost immediately. She was looking directly at me, judging me, and I knew for certain she wouldn't look away at all. Next to her stood Detective Sergeant Alaric Bonthon. He was tall where she was short, broad where she was petite, but she was the one who intimidated police officers when they were suspected of straying outside the lines.

Both were from the Department of Professional Standards. They were the officers assigned to investigate an alleged attack on my partner, DS Ashley Long. Doorbell camera footage, not just from my house but also that of a neighbour across the street, showed me at home during his attack, and that exonerated me. Yet I could see the suspicion still etched into DI Griffiths' face.

A hit and run driver targeted him outside his house eight days ago. I use the word 'targeted' because the incident was considered deliberate. Ashley reported hearing the engine start and the car picking up speed as it came down the street. He realised the danger only at the last moment and his injuries might have been far worse had he not done so.

Left with a broken left ulna, a bad concussion, plus multiple lacerations and contusions, he got off lightly when he leapt to avoid it. He didn't see the driver and suggested the person behind the wheel might have been hiding his face with a hoody, but his cop brain recorded the make, model, and colour of the car.

And the number plate.

It was mine.

The moment he levelled the accusation in my direction, I was placed on administrative leave pending investigation. Now I was standing outside my superintendent's office for a meeting that would allow me to return to work.

Not only had I not run Ashley down, but the car used for the attack wasn't mine. Forensics crawled all over it looking for signs of impact; trace evidence that Ashley would have left as he bounced off the bodywork and glass, but there was none.

They did find his blood on the inside which raised some eyebrows until they spoke with Ashley to confirm what I told them. My partner cut his pinky finger the day before he was

The Truth Will Out

A DS Tony Heaton Cold Case Novel : Book 3

Steve Higgs

Contents

knocked down. I gave him a handkerchief to wrap the wound, but he dripped blood in my car, nevertheless. I found the handkerchief the same evening – he'd dropped it in my car. It was sitting on a shelf in my garage now, where it would remain until I remembered to take it into the house to join the pile of laundry.

The investigating officers accepted I wasn't behind the attack on my partner, and the meeting we now waited to begin was a formality to end my period of administrative leave. However, that did nothing to diminish the hard judgement in DI Griffiths' eyes. She thought I was getting away with something, like I must have had a hand in the attack even though I had an undeniable alibi.

I let a long, slow breath deflate my lungs and tried to push the stress from my muscles.

The door to Superintendent Charters' office opened inward, DCI Harris operating it from the inside where the two men had undoubtedly been discussing my fate. DCI Harris is Ashley's boss and involved only because the report of my involvement was made to him. He'd come gunning for me at the start but offered me a wry smile now.

"Let's get this done, shall we?" boomed the superintendent's voice from inside the office.

I had to follow DI Griffiths and her sergeant inside, making my way toward the boss's desk feeling like a naughty schoolboy sent to see the headmaster.

Less than five minutes later I was coming back out of the door, and the unpleasant affair was in the past and could be forgotten. The meeting was a formality to record the verdict of the professional standards investigation and since my alibi existed in the form of multiple timestamped video recordings, there really wasn't anything to say other than 'case closed'. Despite that, both the team from professional standards and my boss wanted to know why Ashley believed it was me at the wheel.

It wasn't the first time the question had been posed.

I didn't have an answer to give. Or rather, I had an answer, and I wasn't going to give it. My partner had been snooping around an old case of mine. The one that ruined my career. The one that I had worked so hard to keep anyone else from investigating. He suspected me of ... something. I don't think he saw me as Bruce Denton's killer, which of course I am, but maybe as a cop who fiddled with the evidence to hide the truth.

Obviously, I don't really know what he thinks, and I certainly can't ask him without tipping my hand. Bruce Denton had to die and no one else was going to tackle the task, so thirty years ago I took it upon myself to do what no one else would. Then I ruined what would probably have been a glowing career to keep the truth of it hidden. I'm less than two weeks from retirement and have never felt so close to being caught.

DI Griffiths pursued me in the meeting, going back over questions I had already answered more than once. I had no clue why the car used to knock down my partner was the same make, model, and colour as mine. I could offer no explanation as to why the registration Ashley saw was the same as mine, save for weakly pointing out that the poor chap was concussed.

In the end, Superintendent Charters grew bored of her incessant need to pick at me and called the meeting to a close.

Walking away in the direction of the coffee room, though if I'm being honest, it was one of those days when I wished I was carrying a hip flask, I didn't bother to look back. I could feel DI Griffiths' eyes boring into the back of my skull and didn't need to see her slapped backside of a face again anytime soon.

I found Gavin Dobbs, the Herne Bay nick's other detective sergeant, making a round of brews.

"All done and dusted then?" he asked, spooning sugar into five mugs, all of which could do with a clean.

I slumped against the door in an exaggerated way. Disciplinary meetings, even those where you are exonerated, are mentally and emotionally draining.

"Yeah," I sighed, feeling more angry than drained and trying to hide it.

"Want one?" Gavin asked.

I nodded, my mind elsewhere. There was another reason why I didn't give DI Griffiths anything when she grilled me about the doppelganger car. Ashley probably had got the registration wrong, but I was willing to believe his claim that the car used in the attack was the same as mine. And that felt deliberate.

Someone chose to target my partner, and they ran him over with a duplicate of my car. Why? Better yet, who? I could have given Griffiths an answer to both questions, but didn't want to purely on principle. Well, principle and a fervent need to reduce the number of people looking over my shoulder.

Ashley and I met just a few weeks ago when he was assigned to investigate a backlog of unsolved or 'cold' cases. They were almost all murders, but the taskforce put together to deal with it was a political exercise ordered by the Chief Constable for Kent. The counties top officer had people breathing down his neck because a national audit placed us second to bottom on the fail scale.

The taskforce was never expected to net results, but my keener than keen partner saw opportunity in that and boy had he been right. In a surprisingly short amount of time we had solved two historic cases. Cases that would otherwise have never been touched. We were the talk of the town, the chief constable's golden boys, and probably in line for a commendation, if not a medal.

But thus far we had only poked our noses into three cases. With two solved and the appropriate persons now behind bars, that only left one case to consider: the murder of Daniel Mahony. Mahony was a white racist who beat up an old black man. If I can switch to speaking sotto voce for a moment, I think he got what he deserved. But I'm not employed to have an opinion. The law is the law, and someone was responsible for a man's premature death.

The prime suspect was and still is a criminal gang leader called Elroy Stewart. He's the grandson of the old black man Mahony beat up. All the evidence pointed toward Elroy, and I was ready to bet my pension that Elroy Stewart was behind the attack on Ashley. He had form when it came to using a vehicle as a weapon. At least, we believed he did.

Now we just had to prove it.

He was a known criminal, but one who had done very little time behind bars. That meant he was savvy. He owned and ran a legitimate business, a club called The Waterfront, which is located on, um, the waterfront in Whitstable. Undoubtedly a front to hide some of his other activities, he was probably there now where he wouldn't be wasting a single moment thinking about Daniel Mahony.

I took the steaming mug of coffee from Gavin and picked up another so he could avoid a second trip. Leading the way back to the open plan office where we both had desks, I knew I was killing time to delay what had to come next.

The disciplinary investigation dictated that I wasn't allowed to work, but also that I could have no contact with my partner. Now it was officially closed, those rules no longer applied, and I had to return to working alongside my accuser. Now you might think it would be more uncomfortable for him since putting me in the crosshairs turned out to be entirely misguided, and I didn't doubt he would be feeling squeamish and embarrassed to have to apologise. But getting back to work meant getting back to the cases in hand and that meant Bruce Denton. For though our only live case was the unsolved murder of Daniel Mahony in 2003, new evidence, that just happened to come to light at the worst possible time, meant the Bruce Denton case had just been reopened too.

The last thing in the world I wanted was for anyone else to look at it, so when the inevitable happened, I made sure DCI Harris allowed the golden boys first crack. He was amenable. It would work in his favour if we solved another one since he'd been assigned the dubious task of heading the cold case taskforce, but now I had to fight to make sure Ashley didn't discover anything that would lead him to look at me.

I was deep in thought, going back over what I could do or say to explain why I omitted evidence from the official files on the case – Ashley is a bright kid, he would find the holes sooner or later – when I heard someone say his name.

Chapter 2

"Hey, Ashley. You're not dead then," joked Hazel, one of the young constables.

Ashley said something in reply that I didn't catch. A forced smile played across his lips but never made it to his eyes which were now looking at me. There was regret in them, and the concern that I might hold a grudge.

I knew he would feel that way and had been going back and forth about how to best leverage his shame. I wanted him to stop pursuing the Bruce Denton case, but it was too late for that. I wanted him to let me handle it all while he convalesced, but I already knew how that conversation would go. Push too hard and he would become even more suspicious than he already was, so my plan was to do the last thing he expected.

Over the heads of the people in the office, most of whom were sitting, I dipped my head to the right, indicating we should step away. The coffee and break room are down a short corridor that also leads to the restrooms. We needed a little privacy.

Eight days after being knocked down, he was back on his feet but moving with some obvious discomfort. His left lower arm was in a cast and there were a few marks on his head still where scratches had healed but the skin wasn't fully repaired yet.

Able to move faster than him for the first time since we met, I walked ahead, arriving in the break room to await his arrival. He started talking the moment he stepped through the door.

Raising his hands to ward off the attack he assumed was coming, he started to say, "Tony, I know I ..."

But I talked right over the top to stop him. "You did the right thing. What happened isn't your fault."

He performed a sort of double take, hearing my words but then trying to decipher them to see if he'd really heard me right.

I kept talking.

"I think it was deliberate. The use of a car like mine I mean. Someone picked it to mess with our heads, and it was probably Elroy."

Ashley's forehead wrinkled. I had wondered if maybe he was thinking the same thing, but clearly that wasn't the case.

Taking advantage of his momentary surprise, I pressed on. "That's just conjecture, obviously, yet it feels right."

Ashley checked behind him and reversed up to one of the break room tables. He sat awkwardly on one corner, demonstrating his lingering discomfort even as he tried to hide it.

"He does have previous."

I nodded, parking one cheek on another of the tables to reflect his relaxed posture. "That's what I thought. He knows we have reopened the investigation into Daniel Mahony's murder and has no intention of being caught this time either."

Ashley released a slow breath, his eyes unfocused until he looked up at me. "I think the car was supposed to kill me."

I said nothing, but the same thought occurred to me the moment I heard about the incident.

"I was lucky. When I reacted, I jumped in the right direction. Otherwise, I would have been under the wheels and we know how that went for Daniel Mahony."

"Best not to dwell on it," I replied. "Instead, we should nail him."

"We can't. You know that."

"Oh, you mean because his legal team have us over a barrel after what they claim to be a wrongful arrest and police brutality." I pumped my eyebrows and grinned. "Yes, Elroy manoeuvred us very neatly, didn't he. If we go anywhere near him, we will be in hot water, but it just so happens we have another case to investigate in the same area."

Ashley frowned, his eyebrows knitting together as he ran my response through his head.

"Wait. You're talking about ..."

"Bruce Denton? Yes."

His eyebrows unfolded, the confusion he felt clearly displayed.

"Why the change of heart? Simple, dear boy. I have no choice."

Ashley didn't argue. I watched a range of emotions cross his face. From before we met, the Bruce Denton case was the one he wanted to pursue. He'd thought getting teamed with me was the perfect scenario until I fought back so hard, and now I was performing a U-turn to give him precisely what he wanted.

"Look," I said, "We can use the Bruce Denton case to hide our investigation into Elroy Stewart. No one will know."

"I suspect they will."

"Better we get a slap on the wrist than let a dangerous gang leader, drug runner, and murderer walk the streets unimpeded." I knew he couldn't argue with that one. Ashley was a by-the-book obey-the-rules kind of guy, but he was going to have to walk on the wrong side if he wanted to catch Daniel Mahony's killer.

Slumping a little, he said, "Okay, but we have to tread carefully."

"Of course. We wouldn't want anything to tarnish your impeccable record. Oh, wait. You were recently accused of brutality against a person of colour."

Ashley flared his eyes and pointed at his own dark skin.

I gave him a one shoulder shrug. "Like that makes a difference. Elroy is winning. I say we clear your name by taking him down." Emily Harris, who we saw being struck by Elroy in an assault that precipitated his arrest, later stated that her injuries came when Ashley barged into her. Either Elroy held something over her, or she was in his employ. I suspected the former, but she was a link, weak or otherwise, on whom we could lean.

Ashley winced a little when he pushed himself back to upright. "Ok, partner." He offered me his hand to shake. "Let's do it." He kept hold of my hand and held my gaze. "You're really going to help me find Bruce Denton's killer?"

I sucked some air through my nose, nodded, and said, "I am."
Not meaning a single word of it.

Chapter 3

Coming back into the station's main office where we both had desks, we were met by DCI Harris.

"So you are back," he said, speaking to Ashley. "Has the doctor cleared you for work?"

"Yes, sir. I've been working from home, actually, sir. I tried daytime TV but wanted to kill myself by noon on the first day."

We all chuckled politely.

"Which case?" DCI Harris enquired, his voice a little guarded.

We had strict instructions not to go anywhere near Elroy Stewart. After his legal team shredded the whole department and the chief constable heard about it, that came as no surprise, but it was also acknowledged that human nature dictate we want revenge. No one really believed we had chosen to target and brutalise him, but going after him now was dodgy territory.

"Bruce Denton," said Ashley, dutifully. "With the new evidence and the case reopened, we have to see if we can crack it."

I kept my features impassive, but DCI Harris twisted his neck to check what my face said about the decision.

He said, "I thought the video evidence got us nowhere?"

"So far, sir," Ashley confirmed in bright and hopeful tones. "The team have done all they can to enhance the old video footage, but we remain hopeful someone will come forward to identify the woman shown with Bruce Denton and there are other avenues we can pursue."

"Such as?"

Well, Ashley broke into my desk and has a copy of my private file on the Denton case, and he's already discovered I left out a bunch of facts from the official report.

I doubted Ashley was about to reveal that but chose to answer so he couldn't.

"Some of his neighbours are still in the same houses, but even though it's been thirty years, we can track down those who have moved away. It's possible someone will recognise her. I know the video has been shown on the local news, but that's not the same as sticking it under someone's nose and making them really consider if they might know who she is."

DCI Harris gave that some consideration before saying, "Look, I think it's admirable for you to be back at work so soon, Ashley, but don't go overdoing it. These cases have rested this long. A few more days won't hurt."

"I will be sure not to exacerbate my injuries, sir."

Seemingly satisfied, DCI Harris wished us luck. I thought he was going to leave it at that, but he clearly felt he should reinforce the need to respect the restraints placed upon us.

"Now, I'm sure there is no need to remind you," he said, showing that he believed there absolutely was a need, "but stay away from Elroy Stewart. Under no circumstances are you to attempt to clear your names."

He said 'your names' but was looking squarely at Ashley when he said it.

"Have you got that?"

"Loud and clear, sir," said Ashley, dutiful as ever.

DCI Harris shifted his gaze to check with me. "Oh, indubitably," I said.

"Good, because there will be severe consequences if his lawyers can prove you have ignored the terms of your non-molestation order."

Irked by the constant need to tell us what we already knew, and by the lack of backbone displayed, I didn't bother to hide the irritation in my voice when I said, "Yes, we get it."

DCI Harris narrowed his eyes a little and thought about trying to tailor my attitude. Thankfully, for all of us, he recognised the futility in berating a man with no time left to serve. Repeating his good luck message, he let us be. He had three other teams under his command and needed to focus his attention elsewhere. It left us with no reason not to get on with the day. Officially, the world would see us going after Bruce Denton. In secret we would also continue to investigate Elroy Stewart and I didn't give a stuff what his lawyers thought about it.

Had I not been on administrative leave for the last week, I might have already questioned some of the other persons attached to the Daniel Mahony case and would most definitely have organised my life with regards to Bruce Denton's witness list. As it was, all I had done was speak with Vicky Meacock nee Hopper about her conversation with Ashley.

Vicky, a former WPC back when the world was still in the habit of differentiating men and women in the same job, had left the police almost thirty years ago, but knew more about my role in the Bruce Denton investigation than almost anyone else on the planet. She was with me the morning his body was discovered. In the days that followed, she was at my side to help with interviews. With Herne Bay being such a small nick, we only had two detectives and the boss wanted to solve this in house if possible. He assumed the role of senior investigating officer, or SIO, but was never going to do the legwork. I knew that going in.

So Vicky was a problem for me because Ashley sought her out and I had to ask her what she told him without raising her suspicions.

It had proven easier than I expected. We hadn't seen each other in years but had been friendly when our kids were little. She quit not long after the Bruce Denton case was officially closed and was already pregnant at the time.

Two days into my imposed timeout while DI Griffiths and her pack of vultures investigated Ashley's 'accident', I knocked on Vicky's door. Surprised, though not completely, to find me on her doorstep, she invited me in and offered me a beer. Her husband vaguely remembered me but busied himself elsewhere in the house while we talked.

The video of my wife walking arm in arm with Bruce had first aired two days earlier, so Vicky knew the case was being re-opened.

"Any clue who she is?" Vicky had asked.

I recall how I searched her face for any sign that she was leading me into a lie. She knew my wife at the time. She had been to our house. How was it that someone who knew my Mary so well didn't recognise her, even if the video didn't show her face? But Vicky had no idea who the woman with Bruce Denton could be and the sense of relief I felt was almost overwhelming.

Of course my relief was tempered by what she told me about her conversation with Ashley. I always knew she heard and saw things that never made it into the file I compiled. I hid a witness statement that provided a partial number plate because it was for a car I owned at the time. By itself, the VRN wasn't anything to worry about, but any decent detective would add that single clue to another and soon a picture would form. I had worked hard to make sure that snippet was known by no one other than the witness, me, and the person who recorded the statement.

The witness died eight years ago, I was telling no one, but unfortunately for me, the third person was Vicky and short of burning her house down with her inside, there had never been a way to ensure the information would stay buried.

Too late now, it was out.

Vicky had given Ashley her notebooks for the period covering Bruce Denton's murder and while she could tell me roughly what was in them, without seeing them myself, I had no way to prepare lies to defend against questions he might have.

That fact alone led me to broach the subject first. He'd admitted going to see Vicky, so I didn't have to box clever to introduce the subject. As we headed to our desks at the far end of the room, I snapped my fingers as if suddenly remembering something. "Hey, have you got those notebooks Vicky gave you? I wanted to get started on them a week ago, but ..." I didn't need to remind him that his accusation had stopped me from working for the last week.

"Yeah," he said, easing himself into his chair. "They're in my bag. I looked through them again while I was at home and tracked down a couple of the witnesses."

"Oh yeah?" My interest was real.

He leaned down to fetch them from the bag by his feet.

I went to him and once I was close enough to speak at a volume only he would hear, I said, "We should take our show on the road. We can't pursue Elroy from here."

He gave me a nod of acknowledgement and ten minutes later we were leaving the station in my battered old Vauxhall Astra estate. I could have driven his police issue Mondeo, but I like my old jalopy.

In the passenger seat for once, Ashley asked, "Do you have a destination in mind?"

"As a matter of fact, I do."

Chapter 4

IN THE CAR WE discussed what we knew about both cases and what our next steps should be. It was mostly me leading, which, let me tell you, is a step change from the day we first met.

"The black Audi we saw outside Christine Westbury's house belongs to Aldridge Kingston. I pulled his information the day you got run down. I would have got further with it then, but I was in work less than an hour before they sent me home. Aldridge has a record but it's all minor stuff from years ago. A couple of counts of shoplifting, actual bodily harm for three counts when he was a minor ..."

"But not a reformed character. Just someone who worked out how not to get caught."

"That would be my assumption," I replied. We were heading out of Herne Bay, taking the coastal road to Whitstable, but not for the address I had for Aldridge. I had a different destination in mind, one that might shake loose some useful information.

"Where are we going exactly?" Ashley asked, squirming a little in his seat as he tried to get comfortable.

"To visit Emily Harris," I said, checking his reaction in my peripheral vision. "Her lies are why we can't officially investigate Elroy Stewart. Looking back at the incident in the hospital carpark, I have to assume the whole thing was staged. She wasn't there by accident; any more than Elroy was. It's been a week since she gave false testimony, so she will think she has got away with it. I would like to see if we can rattle her cage."

Ashley looked across at me with a concerned expression etched deeply into his face. "You want to visit the woman who claimed I assaulted her?"

I knew why it worried him, but I wasn't about to be put off, so I smiled and said, "Yup."

"Have you looked into her? Is there any connection between her and Elroy?" Ashley's question once again demonstrated his ability to think like a detective.

"Unfortunately not. That would be too easy. It's possible he got to her after the event, threatening her so she lied in her statement. He might even have paid her, but I can't see Elroy parting with money when violence and intimidation are his bedfellows. But going back to what I said about it being staged, he either knows her somehow, like through a mutual friend, or he is holding something over her. The mutual friend thing wouldn't show up when we look for a connection."

"Not unless we got lucky," Ashley agreed.

"But I'd be willing to bet it's the latter, anyway. He's got a hold over her and used that to force her into helping."

Ashley was silent while he thought about it, nodding to accept my thoughts a few moments later.

"You know this could blow up in our faces," he warned. "If she sticks to her guns, our visit could be seen as harassment. Given how she lied the first time, she could claim we tried to make her withdraw her statement."

I gave a kind of half shrug. "That *is* what we are going to try to do."

Ashley exhaled hard and slow, slumping back into his seat. He wasn't wrong that this was a dodgy tactic. Our bosses would not approve. Not even slightly, but there had to be a chink in Elroy's armour, and we wouldn't find it without looking.

We drove in silence for a few minutes, the grey Kent coastline rolling past. I was calculating angles, as always. Confronting Emily served multiple purposes – it might crack open Elroy's network of intimidated witnesses, but more importantly, it would demonstrate to Ashley that I was fully committed to pursuing the case against our chief suspect. The more invested Ashley became in hunting Elroy, the less likely he was to focus his attention on certain inconvenient details from thirty years ago. I knew I couldn't put him off for ever, but a few more days to think about how to deflect or defend against the missing evidence from Bruce Denton's case … well, I needed all the time I could get.

"What's our approach?" Ashley asked as we pulled to the kerb outside Emily's house. She was listed as unemployed, which probably meant she was doing unregistered cash-in-hand work. I didn't know if we would find her at home or not, but it was the best place to start.

"Direct but sympathetic. If we assume she was coerced into lying for Elroy, then she is scared and our arrival will terrify her. Not only will she have Elroy's threats hanging over her head, but she'll fear prosecution from the police if the truth ever comes out. So we offer her protection in exchange for the truth."

I looked up at the house as I stepped out of the car. It was tired, with paint flaking off, bricks missing from the garden wall bordering the street, and litter covering the short path leading to her door. Sadly, it didn't stand out for all the houses in the street were the same.

The front door opened before we could get to it. Light coming from inside framed Emily Harris in the doorway. She looked composed but wary.

"I saw you pull up," she said, her voice steady. "You shouldn't be here."

"Emily," Ashley said gently, "we are here to help." It was a good statement to lead with – our visit wasn't to cause her even more trouble.

However, she crossed her arms as her stance became defensive. "I already gave my statement. I have nothing more to say."

"But we know you lied, Emily," Ashley continued. "What will you do when we prove it?" That wasn't the script we discussed but she wasn't acting as we expected.

Emily's expression hardened. "You barged into me during the chase. I was hurt because of your recklessness."

"Emily, please," I interjected. "You don't have to protect him."

"Protect him?" She let out a short laugh. "I'm protecting myself by telling the truth. DS Long was out of control. I witnessed the rage on his face. He was so focussed on tackling that poor man that I don't think he even noticed I was there."

Her ability to lie was frustratingly convincing. It was as though she genuinely believed what she said.

I tried a different approach. "Emily, Elroy Stewart is dangerous. He's hurt other people. If he's threatening you—"

"Nobody's threatening me," she cut me off sharply. "I don't know why you can't accept that your partner made a mistake, but I won't be harassed into changing my story."

"This isn't harassment," Ashley said. "We're trying to understand …"

"Understand what? That police officers sometimes get carried away? That innocent people get hurt when you lot decide to play heroes?"

I placed a hand on Ashley's shoulder, a silent indication that I wanted him to stay quiet for a moment. Holding Emily's eyes with my own, I let mine bore into hers. My ability to tell when a person is lying would do me no good today because I already knew she was. But could I figure out why?

"He has something on you," I stated flatly, watching her face to see how she reacted.

Emily didn't exactly twitch, but her lips moved when a response formed only to be bitten down.

"No," I gave a small shake of my head. "That's not quite right, is it? Elroy is manipulating you because that's what he does, and you really believe that we can't help."

A tear formed in her right eye and there it was, the confirmation I needed.

Making my words the vocal equivalent of a warm hug, I said, "What is it, Emily? If you did something that he is threatening to expose, we can take it into consideration." I was guessing, playing the odds to figure out what it could be that would convince her to lie like this.

She swiped at the tear, pushing it away and taking control once more.

Knowing she was about to speak, I tried again. "Is it a family member?" I thought about what Helen Hoath-Salter said about her mum and daughter. "If he's threatened to hurt someone, we can use that to put him away."

I expected her to argue about his lieutenants, the same way Helen did, but yet again I had misjudged her.

Sounding just a little bit broken, Emily was almost too quiet to hear when she said, "You can't help me." Her eyes were down, refusing to meet ours. "I've said all I'm going to say. Now please leave my property."

Ashley said, "Emily, I know this is difficult, but—"

Flicking her head up defiantly, her demeanour changed yet again. Now growling, even though I could see the pain in her eyes, she said, "The only thing that's difficult is having two police officers turn up at my door trying to intimidate me into lying." She stepped back and grabbed the door. "Don't come here again."

"Wait!" I called out, but the door slammed shut with finality.

Neither of us moved for a beat, our eyes still staring at the spot where she had been standing.

Voicing my thoughts, I said, "That didn't go as I hoped."

Ashley snorted in an amused but annoyed manner. "That's an understatement."

I took out my contact card. It's rare for people to call the number on them, but we are encouraged to hand them out anyway.

Raising my voice a little so she would hear it, I said, "Emily, I'm putting my card through the door." I posted it through the letterbox. "Please call me if you have anything you want to get off your chest. Anything at all. We can help." I reinforced what I believed to be true.

Dropping his voice to a whisper as we turned away and walked back to the car, Ashley said, "If she reports this …"

"We'll be deep in the doodoo," I finished his sentence. There was nothing we could do about it. "She's not just refusing to help; she's actively working against us."

"And I want to know why." Ashley paused on his side of the car. "I thought you had her there for a moment."

"I did too. Whatever Elroy is using to keep her in check is clearly very effective."

"But what could Elroy possibly have on her to make her this committed to the lie?"

I started the engine, my mind already working through possibilities. "That's what we need to find out. Emily Harris doesn't strike me as someone who'd normally tangle with organized crime. So what's her connection to Elroy?"

As we drove away, I glanced in the rearview mirror and saw a curtain fall back into place. She watched us leave and I questioned if all she needed was some time for our words to sink in.

Chapter 5

OUR FIRST INTERVIEW WAS a failure, but that's just how police work goes. Maybe Emily would come around, and perhaps with a little research we would be able to figure out why she lied for Elroy. Our next stop was Rachael Weaver, an old lady who identified Elroy in a line up more than two decades ago. She lived on the other side of the ancient seaside resort and not far from Christine Westbury who we spoke to more than a week ago.

The question wasn't so much whether Elroy had visited Rachael to ensure she knew to keep her mouth shut, but whether he still had someone watching her. Aldridge, his car at least, had been parked in the street near Christine's house when we got there and the poor woman had been terrified. But did Elroy believe we were off the case and would stay away? And if so, did that mean he'd withdrawn his forces? I reckoned that would be the case, not least because staking out an old lady for a week would be boring in the extreme.

I drove along Harbour Street, passing fishing boats coming back in from their early morning ventures or already in the quay offloading their catch. The scent of the sea came through the car's vents, making my nose wrinkle.

Turning onto High Street, we slowed to allow for pedestrians stepping into the road as they passed one another because the pavements are so narrow, and for the traffic calming bumps, there to reduce the likelihood of anyone (specifically tourists who gawp at the architecture and drink too much in the summer) getting knocked down. We climbed the hill leading out of the town to the motorway but turned right onto St David's Close to arrive outside Mrs Weaver's house a few minutes before noon.

My stomach was just beginning to signal its desire to be filled but it would have to wait until we were done here.

Mrs Weaver owned a double fronted, two storey detached house with a large front garden. The street had a row of similar properties, most of which boasted mature shrubbery and well planted borders. In contrast to Emily's place, Mrs Weaver kept her house spotless. Even from the street I could tell the windows were clean on both sides. I imagined her to be a tough old bird with a routine that included housework every day and home cooked food. She was a widow, that much I had checked already, and I expected to find her at home.

So I was a little put out when no one answered the door.

Ashley peered through a window. Cupping his hands around his face to cut out the light, he reported, "I can see through the living room and into the kitchen. I don't see any movement."

I took myself to the window on the other side of the front door and looked for myself. The room was an office. There were books on shelves along one wall and a desk positioned so the person inside would be able to look at the front garden and the street beyond. There was no sign of life.

Ashley asked, "Want to check around the back?"

A sense of dread squirmed its way through my gut, replacing the growing hunger with something much worse.

To the right of the house, a tall gate set into a brick arch led to the back garden. Seeing no padlock on the other side, I operated the latch and stepped through. The back garden was just like the front, which is to say it had been nurtured and sculpted by a caring hand. In November we were not seeing it at its best and I could only imagine how vibrant and colourful it might look in the summer.

I observed it all without comment, making my way around the side of the house to access the rear façade. A centre set patio led to a pair of doors. They were locked and there was no sign of anyone inside.

Ashley joined me in looking through the windows. Peeking inside people's homes felt like prying when I first donned the uniform, but I got over it a long time ago. Half expecting to find the old lady collapsed on the floor, I was relieved to find no sign of her. Of course, collapsed would have been my preference over the darker alternative. That Elroy might eliminate a potential witness had crept into my thoughts unbidden when she failed to open the door, but my worries were for naught.

"It's Tuesday, so she's not collecting her pension," I said.

Murmuring his response in a distracted manner, Ashley said, "No one 'collects' their pension anymore, Tony. Pensioners these days can manage to use online banking like the rest of the planet."

I wanted to argue and knew I would be right to assert that not all pensioners were technology savvy, but regardless, Mrs Weaver wasn't at the post office behind a queue of eager old people.

We made our way back to the front of the house to find a couple in their sixties looking nervous and trying to pretend they hadn't been watching what we were doing. They weren't dressed to be outdoors, and I suspected I would find they were wearing house slippers if I looked at their feet. It told me all I needed to know.

"It's okay," I called out before they could hurry away. I held up my warrant card. They were concerned neighbours who saw two men climb out of a battered old car and then proceed to let themselves around the back of someone's house. I applauded their decision to investigate.

Seeing the obvious relief on their faces, I tucked my identification away but continued walking until I joined them in the street.

"Detective Sergeant Heaton at your service. Any idea where Mrs Weaver could be?"

"Rachael?" said the woman. "She's not home then?"

A dozen flippant responses filled my mind, but her husband got in first.

"Of course she's not home, you daft old bag. Why else would the police be asking if we know where she is?"

The woman glared at her husband, who was looking at me and rolling his eyes as if to say, 'Women'. I wisely opted to give no reaction or response.

"Does she have friends she meets with? Or a group she attends, perhaps at a local church?"

The man opened his mouth to speak, and his wife ever so deliberately stepped in front of him to get my attention and stand on his toes. He yanked his foot away when she crushed his toes and glared at the back of her head, but she was already talking.

"Not that I know of. She has a daughter who visits a few times a week. She lives in Herne Bay and she's a nurse, but I didn't see if she was here this morning. They go out for lunch sometimes."

"I don't suppose you know her name?"

Ashley had joined me in the street, listening to what they had to say.

"Oh, yes," the woman was happy to be able to provide answers. "Rachael's daughter is Cindy Gunderson. She's divorced now but kept the name."

Her husband had recovered from having his toes squashed, but chose, or perhaps knew well enough, to keep his mouth shut.

Ashley stepped away to speak with dispatch. If Cindy lived locally, we could get an address and probably a home phone number. We might even get a place of work and mobile. There was no desperate need to speak with Mrs Weaver, and I didn't hold out much hope that we would get a result from her, but

I wanted to be able to pin down her location so we wouldn't waste another trip.

Ten minutes later we were in my car and had nothing to show for our morning, save for the fact that we were actively back on the case. We had an address for Cindy, but no mobile number and she wasn't answering her home phone.

Drawing a blank so far on the Daniel Mahony case, we put it to one side to focus instead on Bruce Denton.

Chapter 6

"You seem surprisingly okay with this." Ashley observed as we made our way back through Whitstable.

I assumed he was referring to the fake panic attacks I have employed in the past to divert him away from the subject.

Shrugging my shoulders in a resigned fashion, I said, "I'm trying to come to terms with it. It's happening either way, so I might as well get on board. It's that or curl up in a corner and miss out on the chance to finally solve this thing." I consciously kept my eyes on the road. I was lying through my teeth and didn't need him to see what my features were doing.

If he felt like challenging me, he chose not to. Or put it off until later.

"You think we might solve it? Since the day I met you, you've never once changed your tune that the case is unsolvable."

I shrugged again. "There's new evidence, though." I meant the video they dug out of the bog, but the moment the words left my mouth I saw my mistake.

"Yes, I've been meaning to talk to you about that."

The video showed my wife, but since no one had come forward in more than a week to say they recognised her, it might as well have shown Greto Garbo. I was probably off the hook on that one, but Ashley had spoken to at least one of the other officers involved in the case at the time and I couldn't be sure how much he now knew.

"Go on," I encouraged, trying not to sound guarded.

"I told you I spoke with Vicky, right?"

"Yes. I spoke with her too. She said she gave you copies of her notes from the time, and you said there was information in them that never made it into the official case file."

"That's right," said Ashley, sounding surprised. "You went to see her?"

"Yes." I looked his way for the first time in more than a minute. "You were in hospital and then at home. I was on administrative leave and barred from talking to you. I couldn't work officially, but I could visit an old friend. I hadn't thought about Vicky or spoken her name out loud in years until you brought her up the other day. I wanted to know what it was that I missed."

"And?" Ashley prompted me to keep talking.

"And nothing, really. She gave you the copies she had of her notes, so I haven't been able to read them. She told me what she remembered, but it was thirty years ago." I was having to be so careful with what I said. I couldn't bring up any of the things I was supposed to not know unless Vicky told me about them when we spoke a few days ago. Ashley was bound to check back with her at some point. Looking back at it now, I should have buried everything in her notes, not just the parts that alluded to the man in the car. Including some of it and not the rest was far more suspicious than just leaving it all out. I had to hope Ashley didn't ask me how that came to be.

"Don't you think it's odd that some of the information she recorded ended up in the case file but not all of it?"

Nuts.

"I wish I had an answer for how that came about. I wish I could go back and have her notes thirty years ago. Would they have made a difference? We'll never know, but I agree that it's odd."

Ashley was quiet for a few moments, undoubtedly thinking about what to say next. Not for the first time, I questioned whether I should ask him why he broke into my desk. Doing so would put all the cards on the table and allow us to discuss what was in the file I had maintained all these years, but it would also force me to answer questions about why certain elements of the case had been left out. I wasn't entirely confident I could pull that off without slipping up and chose to continue to ignore his invasion of my privacy.

When Ashley spoke again, it was to say, "What do you make of the lack of evidence at the crime scene?"

This, at least, was one question I had anticipated.

"You're talking about the complete absence of fingerprints, hair, fibre, DNA, or anything whatsoever from the killer. That's assuming the blonde woman wasn't responsible."

"Forensic analysis deemed it unlikely a woman would be able to generate the force employed in the attack unless she was particularly tall and muscular. Certainly the woman in the video is too slight, so yes, if we believe the killer is a man, he managed to perpetrate the attack without leaving a trace. How did he do that?" Ashley was probing. He'd read the case file and knew the conclusions made at the time.

"There remains the possibility that he just got lucky, but that's not what you are asking, is it? You want to know if I side with the theory that the killer could have been someone from law enforcement."

"Could it?"

Absolutely.

I sighed and said, "I don't know. I didn't want to believe it at the time, and I guess I still don't. It would fit, though. Someone with a deep knowledge of crime scenes or forensic science could have pulled it off." My mind raced. Was I putting myself into the frame as a suspect? It felt like I was lining up the crosshairs on my own head. If I said the wrong thing now, it would be like pulling the trigger.

"Vicky said that one of your colleagues really pushed the idea. How seriously was it taken at the time? I mean, was there anyone who could have fit the bill?"

Seeing an opportunity to kill the subject, I snapped, "Of course there wasn't! I ... *we* explored every possibility back then. You know how many years of my life have gone into this case. If I thought the killer could have been one of the guys at the nick or even at one of the other nicks in the area, don't you think I would have investigated it?"

Ashley narrowed his eyes a little. He wasn't used to being shouted at.

Calming, I said, "The person who first raised it was the other DS in Herne Bay. He expected to get the case because he was the senior guy. I had only just been promoted, but he was busy on another investigation, and I swooped. Back then I still thought I was going places. I gave the cop-as-the-killer concept credence because I had to, not because I really believed it."

I thought Ashley would move on and he did, but not in a good way.

"Why do you think the thief ditched the camcorder in a bog?"

The question caught me by surprise, and I felt bile rising. My hands were instantly clammy on the steering wheel, and I questioned if the colour had just drained from my face. Did I look guilty now? I sure felt it.

I invented the story of the thief in the minutes after I saw my wife on the piece of video footage. I knew I had to destroy it, but the call about it had come through the station's dispatch desk so I couldn't just throw it away. The guys at the nick were waiting for me to bring it back and it sounded like a real breakthrough. But when I launched it into the soggy quagmire it never once occurred to me that it might ever be found. What thief would steal a thing and then drive miles from anywhere to discard it? At the time, a camcorder, a new one at that, was worth a few quid. It was sealed inside an evidence bag, but that wouldn't have put anyone off. If I had just removed it from the damned bag, I wouldn't be in this position today. I had never realised how dodgy and unlikely it looked until Ashley posed the question.

Since I hadn't spoken, Ashley said, "I've been trying to figure out why they would throw it away. They went to the trouble of stealing it only to dump it without even opening the bag it was in. We can be sure they didn't because the seals never work twice, and it managed to keep the water out for thirty years."

Scrambling for words, I said, "I guess they must have freaked out when they realised they'd taken it from a cop."

"Why? Why would that bother them?"

"Depends who they were. It might have been a couple of kids making their first snatch. They think they can make a few easy bucks until they realise it's in an evidence bag. Then they worry selling it on will bring the police to their doors. We're never going to know."

Ashley had been half twisted in his seat to converse with me but shuffled his backside around to look out through the windscreen again. "It's still odd that it was so far from Herne Bay where they nicked it."

I agreed and prayed the discussion was over.

Chapter 7

I DROVE US TO Bruce's street with my heart still hammering in my chest. I felt lightheaded and wanted to lie down but had to act as though nothing was wrong. I couldn't keep faking panic attacks, not when I'd already told Ashley I was doing okay.

"This is the one?" Ashley asked, peering through the window on his side. I had pulled to the kerb right outside Bruce's house.

To me it at once looked completely different and exactly the same as it always had. The doors and windows were different, a garage had been added to one side, and where there was once a hedge which conveniently concealed my wife's face when Bruce led her down the path to his house, there was nothing now. Yet the same feeling I always get when I look at his house stole back through my subconscious.

I flexed my fingers, both hands still on the steering wheel. It wasn't hard to act unnerved and off balance. It wasn't an act at all. Both things were true.

Ashley's question caught up with me, and I frowned when I looked at him. "You haven't been here before?"

"Nope. I thought about it, but there was always something else to do. Plus, I figured you would come around eventually, and it would be better for me if the first time I saw it was with your eyes. Can you walk me through it?"

"The crime scene and the investigation?" At least I was on solid ground doing that. I released my death grip on the wheel and stepped out.

Ashley exited onto the pavement where I joined him in staring at the house. There were new people living there now, a family called the Thomsons. I hadn't met them and saw no need to remind them of the grisly murder that took place in their home.

The property lay vacant for three years after the murder. Ownership fell to Bruce's parents because he had no will and no other relatives and I guess they couldn't find the energy or emotional balance to deal with it. Eventually, it was bought by a builder who gutted the inside and brought the décor up to date.

Three owners had occupied it since then. The Thomsons were just the most recent.

Of all the people connected to the case who I had talked to over the years, it was only Bruce's parents that I felt sorry for. They had no idea why their son had been killed, and I couldn't tell them. I have never regretted what I did, not even a little bit, but when I saw their pain, it messed with my sleep and made me feel bad about myself.

It was the price I had to pay.

I talked Ashley through the call I intercepted at the dispatch desk. I'd known it would be coming and had to make sure I got the case. Not that I told him that part. Recalling it all vividly, I told him how hot it was that day, how all the neighbours spilled onto the street or stood on their front stoops to watch the drama unfold.

"Bryan Hayworth, the other DS at the Herne Bay nick, arrived in the early afternoon offering to help. He'd been dealing with a burglary that morning, one of a recent spate that were believed to be the work of the same person. He caught the guy a few weeks later, but on that day he knew murder trumped theft. I thought he would make a fuss about me taking the case, but he didn't. In fact, he was unexpectedly helpful until I realised he was waiting for me to mess up. He wanted to be able to say he'd done all he could to guide and act as a mentor, but really he was just looking for the boss to recognise I was out of my depth."

"Were you?"

A light snort of air left my nose at Ashley's directness.

"I didn't think so, but that's what my boss came to believe. When Bryan introduced the idea of the killer being someone from law enforcement, it upset everyone, but the superintendent insisted we consider it. The crime scene was incredibly clean."

Walking along the street, I pointed out where Mrs Davenport had lived. "She's the one who reported the man sitting in his car." I made sure Ashley understood the relevance.

"But not the only one. There were three reports given by different people."

That was the point I wanted him to raise. "Precisely. Three reports from three people, each with a completely different car and vastly different descriptions of the man sitting inside it."

"They're not that different," Ashley argued. "They all reported a white male sitting in a car. The oldest age given for the suspect was maybe thirties. I read the reports myself. The man in the car with a registration ending F-U-N was believed to be in his twenties. That narrows the field considerably. He would be in his mid to late fifties now. Early sixties at a push."

Bang on.

I shook my head, dismissing the notion. "I think that's a red herring. We followed up the reports at the time, and do you know what we found?"

"Enlighten me."

"Nothing. The descriptions were too vague. None of the witnesses could be specific about what car they had seen, and they ranged in colour from red to black to possibly silver maybe grey. The man either had long blonde hair, or it was short and brown. He might have had a beard or a moustache, but they couldn't agree on that either. I genuinely believe we were looking at three or more separate men who could have been in the street for any reason."

"But you didn't know about the F-U-N plate," Ashley hastened to point out, reminding me, as if that were necessary, that I never recorded the information in the official case file. "It's only a partial, but we also have a colour and a possible make and model. That's going to help us narrow it down."

"That's assuming she didn't get it wrong."

"Are you saying we should ignore it?"

I ran out of argument. I knew exactly what make and model it was because it was my car. In the days leading up to his murder, I staked out Bruce's property multiple times to identify his pattern of movement. Each time I used a car from the impound lot. No one ever checked them, and the keys were hung on hooks in an unmanned office. Except that one day when I couldn't get one and told myself it would be fine if I used my own car.

It wasn't.

The mere suggestion that we should ignore Mrs Davenport's report would be highly suspicious. I was going to promote the idea that I would look into it when movement caught our attention.

"I thought that was you," said Valerie Smith.

I had already turned my head to look, but seeing who it was, I shifted my feet so I faced her. She was coming down the path of the house next-door-but-one to Bruce. She was in her mid-sixties now, and divorced from the one man we arrested in the days following the murder.

Meeting with the garden gate between us, I shook her hand and said, "Hello, Val."

"You're not still investigating, are you?" she asked, probably knowing I was, but filled with disbelief all the same.

"I'm afraid to say the case has been reopened." As her eyebrows rose in surprise, I introduced my partner. "This is Detective

Sergeant Ashley Long. He's ... well, I was about to say he's helping me, but in truth it's probably the other way around."

Ashley shook her hand when she offered it.

"Valerie was married to Trevor Smith who you will recall was arrested at the time."

Ashley nodded and address Mrs Smith, "Your daughter was a pupil at the school where Mr Denton taught, is that right?"

"Yes. She had something of a crush on poor Bruce, but that's all it was."

Jumping in, I explained, "Mr Smith came home to find me in his kitchen with his wife. Vicky was upstairs talking to Poppy – that's Valerie's daughter. He became quite angry and threatened violence. The arrest was necessary, and he had a prior from a bar fight in his youth."

For a while I had wondered if I could pin the murder on him. If I falsified just a few pieces of evidence, I would have been able to make it look like he believed his fifteen-year-old daughter was sleeping with Bruce and took matters into his own hands. Poppy wasn't doing anything of the sort but that wouldn't matter. But just as I was putting something together and telling myself the family would be so much better off without him, Valerie provided him with an alibi.

Ashley had already asked me about Trevor weeks ago when we first discussed the case, so he knew why Valerie's ex-husband was never charged. Valerie left him a few years later when her daughter moved out, but there was no need to bring that up today.

"I saw the video of Bruce and that blonde on the local news," said Valerie. "Has anyone come forward to identify her?"

The question was aimed at me, so I answered. "Not so far, but we are keeping our fingers crossed." I wasn't doing any such thing.

As though confused by my dogged persistence after so many years, she frowned when she asked, "Do you really think you will catch the killer this time?"

I gave her an exaggerated shrug. About my tenth of the day. "We won't if we don't try." It was a good catch-all response that was as accurate as it was meaningless.

Valerie wished us luck and said goodbye to Ashley and then me. Her farewell sounded a little wistful to my ears.

For the next half an hour, I talked Ashley through the case some more, my trip down memory lane filled with poignant half remembered snippets of conversations with people who were no longer alive. It was one of the things that went in my favour. Something like half the people we talked to in the days and weeks following the murder were no longer with us. Thirty years will do that to a mature population. There were plenty left we could talk to, but they were nothing to worry about. My years of following up the case had been for one simple reason: to ensure there were no new memories.

Ashley could speak to whomever he wanted because they wouldn't be able to tell him anything that would lead him back to me. It was only the video that hung over my head like a giant weight ready to drop. Well, that and Mrs Davenport's partial registration.

If there was anything else out there that could incriminate me, I didn't know what it was. And that scared me.

Chapter 8

ARRIVING BACK AT THE nick in Herne Bay, we had a few hours of shift left to complete and a whole truck load of research to complete. Mindless, boring hours hunched over a computer is steady fodder for a police detective, but we couldn't easily investigate Elroy Stewart at the nick where someone might spot that we were delving into a case we'd been expressly forbidden from touching.

And therein lay an opportunity.

Clearly nowhere near one hundred percent, I suggested Ashley take his work home where he would be more comfortable. Knowing he would resist, I leaned closer so I could whisper, "You can't be seen looking into Elroy here."

Twisting his head to meet my eyes, he understood what I was saying.

"What about Bruce?

"You go. I've got this. I'll start on that partial registration search. That's going to spew a whole load of results, so I'll be tied up going through that line by line for the rest of the day. Unless you really want to do it?" I dangled the hook, certain he wouldn't bite.

"Hell, no. You can have it, but send me the results, okay?"

He wanted to check my work. I said, "Sure," and walked him to his car instead of into the nick. "Early start tomorrow?" I offered, feigning a desire to put in extra hours.

I got a grin in reply. One that told me he thought he was winning. He was the young, dynamic guy with a career trajectory that would take him to the very top. When we met I was so over the hill and impossible to motivate it had pained him to be partnered with me, yet here I was acting like a changed man.

If only he knew the truth.

"I'll be here for 0730hrs," he said, slipping behind the wheel of his unmarked Ford Mondeo.

"Yeah, well, I'll see you at eight. I'm not that keen." I tapped the roof of his car and stepped away, waving him off before I made my way inside.

At my desk, I took my time, making a coffee and checking in with Mary before accessing the central database to look for the

... well, to look for my old car. I won't bore you with how the system works, and in truth it's grown too technologically advanced for me to know anymore, but I can key in a partial plate, a few other details such as likely year – for which I put 'prior to 1994' and send the tiny squirrels that live inside the computer to go search.

If you live under a rock and somehow don't know this stuff, the format for number plates in the UK changed in 2001. Prior to that they indicated the year with a letter, not a number, and obscurely the letter changed each year on August 1st. In 1993, any car not wearing a private plate followed a simple pattern: A letter to indicate the year of first registration, three random numbers and then three random letters.

Every car was the same regardless of make or model and mo-torbikes were no different. That the random letters might spell a three-letter word was a mathematical probability. Sometimes the first letter would play along and on very rare occasions even the numbers would help to form a longer word if one looked at it a bit squint and allowed the word to be tortured into shape.

Regardless, I was looking for F-U-N and knew I was going to get a whole stack of hits because, for whatever reason, there were lots of cars in our area at that time with that particular com-bination. That claim gives rise to argue that the letters weren't random at all, but I don't want to get into that.

Computers being what they are, it needed about two seconds to generate a result.

It presented me with a list on which I could then perform further searches to reduce the number of entries. The first list was national, so I refined it for the county which cut the number by more than ninety percent. I was left with more than two hundred results.

Knowing what I was looking for in advance made it easy, so I scanned row by row until I found the entry for my car. It was necessary to click on each entry to see details about the make and model, the date first registered, the registered keeper, and their address. I was listed halfway down page three.

Taking a breath to steady my nerves – the sight of my car on the page felt like a spectre looking over my shoulder – I noticed something that made me choke out a laugh.

I wasn't the registered keeper. Mary was!

It was so long ago that I'd completely forgotten that little fact. For the life of me I couldn't recall why we put it in her name, but it was probably to make the insurance cost less by having her as the named driver. That sounded right. It was my job that made my insurance bracket higher. I could remember being angry about it now and how one of my superiors told me how he got around it.

This was going to be so much simpler than I expected!

We were looking for a man, so it stood to reason that I would refine the search to eliminate women, plus all those men who fell way outside of the age bracket. The reports regarding men seen in their cars in the street listed the age as either twenties or thirties. I could have taken out everyone over forty. Or at least over forty-five, but I chose to include everyone up to sixty. I wanted Ashley to have a stack of potential suspects to sift. The more time he spent going through the list, the less time he would have for anything else on this case. Yes, I wanted him to get to the point where he felt all possible leads were exhausted, but I also wanted him exhausted at that point.

Cross referencing a long list of people would go a long way to achieving that aim.

By the time I had finished filtering the list, there were only sixty-three names remaining, but for each one my partner would have to cross reference the name against what we knew about Bruce Denton, searching for something that might connect them. Not that there was anything to connect me with the murder victim, aside from the small fact that I killed him and then investigated his death.

Anyway, at just shy of five o'clock, I attached the list to an email and sent it to Ashley along with my findings. If he chose to do the search himself and thought to look at the women as well, he would catch me in a heartbeat. The inclusion of 'Mary Heaton' on the list would stand out like a sore thumb to someone like my partner. Ashley would delve a little deeper, leap to an obvious conclusion and I would be sunk. But I couldn't envisage a scenario in which he would ever think to check the women.

With the email sent, I shut down my computer and packed my bag. I could help Ashley explore the names later and would be happy to do so because I doubted any of them would have any connection to the man I murdered. All the same, there was a tremble in my fingers from the adrenaline raging around my bloodstream.

Thinking my racing pulse needed a few healthy shots of whisky to calm it, I packed my things and headed home.

Chapter 9

ASHLEY HAD RESISTED TAKING painkillers for the last three days, despite his discomfort, because he wanted his head clear. He also liked to know what his base pain level was, and the painkillers masked it. He was uncomfortable, that was all. The broken arm was healing, and the bruises, which hurt far worse than the snapped ulna in the beginning, had subsided into the background. They only hurt if he poked them.

Apart from his right hip.

Leaping to get clear of the onrushing car, he hadn't quite made it, and his right side caught the brunt of the impact. The doctors said the ball of his hip impacted the inside of the socket with enough force that the soft tissue inside the socket was bruised. Walking had been painful. Now it was just annoying and more than anything he was bored with being injured. He wouldn't actually do it, but he longed to rip the cast off his arm and go to the gym.

Home early for once, which still felt like skiving even though he brought his work with him and would continue to work way past his allotted shift hours, he settled into the reclining chair in the corner of the living room and opened his laptop.

The task was to prove Elroy Stewart murdered Daniel Mahony. Robert 'Bobby' Lamson was one way they might begin to unpick the lies. When they first quizzed him, more than a week ago now, Tony tricked him into tripping over his own words. He told them there was no one else in the car, which was as good as saying Elroy was behind the wheel and not where he and multiple alibis claimed him to be.

His whereabouts at the time of the murder were corroborated by a photograph. Twenty years ago, people were still using digital cameras. Even though most phones had a camera in them by then, the quality was still poor. The photograph in question had a convenient (surely, deliberate) time stamp on it.

For now the photograph was a dead end, so Ashley focused on the witnesses instead. Two women, Rachael Weaver and Christine Westbury, challenged the authenticity of the photograph when they recorded statements they later withdrew. Helen Hoath-Salter had presented another opportunity to prove Elroy and his lieutenants lied in 2003, but like Christine Westbury, she was also too scared to provide a truthful statement now.

Ashley doubted Rachael would be any different, but that was no good reason not to try her again. Checking his emails to make sure he had the right number, he dialled her home phone. It was almost five and he expected that she would be home from whatever it was that drew her from the house.

"Hello?" The voice coming down the line was not what he expected. It was strong and young when he expected something older, but it also sounded tired as though beaten down by life.

"Good afternoon," Ashley replied. "This is Detective Sergeant Long of Kent Police calling for Rachael Weaver."

The person at the end took a small breath as though about to speak, only to then pause as if suddenly questioning why the police would be calling.

"Is that you, Mrs Weaver?" Ashley prompted.

"Sorry," the voice replied. "No, I'm her daughter, Cindy. Can I ask what this is about?" Her concern was normal and natural. Ashley heard the same from innocent people all the time. The moment a police officer speaks to them, they assume they have done something wrong.

"I'm investigating an old case your mother is connected to. She gave a statement in 2003 ..."

"2003?"

"Yes. The case has been reopened, and I just need to speak with your mother as a matter of routine." Ashley chose to play it down. If he could convince Mrs Weaver to change her statement, her involvement would be anything but routine. "Is she there?"

"Who is it, love?" The slightly wobbly voice of an older lady echoed in the background.

Ashley heard Cindy take her mouth away from the phone to say, "It's the police, Mum. Nothing to worry about." Responding to Ashley's question, Cindy said, "I'm sorry, but mum isn't well. At all. She has cancer and I've been at the hospital with her today for another bout of chemotherapy."

"This won't take more than a few moments of her time." Ashley sympathised but wasn't about to be put off. Catching Daniel Mahony's killer was important.

"Can't it wait until the morning? I need to feed her some dinner and get her to bed. The chemo always leaves her exhausted."

"This really won't take more than a minute or so." *Unless she is willing to change her statement.*

Clearly unhappy about it but with her mum's voice now coming through louder to make Ashley think she had come to the phone, Cindy conceded.

"Hello?" said Rachael Weaver. Ashley could imagine the elderly lady sitting on a dining chair with the phone clutched in both hands. "Is this about Daniel Mahony?"

Relieved that he could avoid a long explanation, Ashley introduced himself and got to the point. "Mrs Weaver, I wish to speak to you about the statement you gave and then withdrew in 2003." He would have continued but Mrs Weaver had started to talk.

"Has the case reopened? A pair of young men came to my door a week ago. No, it was ten days, I think. Black men they were."

Ashley noted a hint of racism in her tone but let it pass.

"They said I was to make sure I didn't speak to the police about what I thought I saw in 2003."

"What?" squawked Cindy, her voice now the one in the background. "Mum, you didn't tell me about this. Who were they?"

"Mrs Weaver," Ashley jumped in quickly. "Can you describe the two men?"

"Well, they were both black." The hint of racism was back. "They were quite threatening, actually. I told them to go away and one of them tried to grab my arm."

"Mum!" Cindy continued to interrupt.

"I think they might be the same young men that threatened me the first time. Well, I say threatened me, but it was Cindy they said they would hurt."

"What!" This was all news to Cindy.

"Mrs Weaver," Ashley almost held his breath when he posed the question he wanted to ask, "are you prepared to change the statement you gave in 2003?"

"You mean change it back? Yes, I think I will. I don't like being threatened and I'm far too old and sick to care about what they think they can do to me."

Gritting his teeth and fighting to not grunt his discomfort, Ashley levered himself out of the armchair. "Mrs Weaver, I'm going to come to you. I can be there by," he shot his cuff to check the time, then calculated average speed at this time of the day, "six o'clock." She could identify the men who came to her door, and he was certain they would be associates of Elroy's, but that was small stuff compared to her willingness to tell the truth. If she claimed she changed her statement under duress, it would blow the case wide open. It might not be enough to convince the crown prosecution service to move forward, but it would get things moving in the right direction.

Away from the phone, Cindy and her mother were arguing. Ashley was on his feet and rethinking his painkiller policy. If a couple of tablets took the edge off the stiffness in his hip, the slight dulling of his senses would be worth it.

The front door opened, the sound of Tanya returning home reaching Ashley's ears as he tried to wrap up his phone conversation.

"Mrs Weaver?" he went to the front door where Tanya was stepping out of her heels. "Mrs Weaver?" he tried again, using his free arm to hold the wall while he slipped his feet back into his shoes.

Tanya cupped his chin and kissed the side of his face as she headed deeper into the house.

Abruptly, the conversation between mother and daughter ended and Cindy's voice was back in his ear.

"I'm sorry, but I cannot allow you to come here tonight. As my mother's primary carer, I must insist that she rests. Honestly, she will probably be asleep before you can get here and I need to make sure she is in bed, not one of the armchairs, before that happens. You can speak with her in the morning. In fact, I can bring her to you at the station in Whitstable."

Ashley grimaced. He wanted to go now. Having heard Mrs Weaver's conviction, he doubted she was going to change her mind overnight, but his need to record what she had to say made him want to push. He wanted to go despite Cindy's advice. Maybe the traffic would be light and he would get there quicker than expected. He even opened his mouth to say that he was on his way and was happy to kneel beside her bed to ask questions, when Cindy spoke again.

"What time shall I arrive? I have to get mum up in the mornings and she's slow these days. I can probably be with you by eleven."

Ashley released a slow breath and told himself to cool his jets. Following the assault charge on Elroy, even if it was bogus, and having pushed Emily Harris hard enough today that she could legitimately file a harassment complaint, the last thing he needed was to be overzealous with a sick old lady suffering from cancer.

"It's Herne Bay, Mrs Gunderson. I'm working out of the station in Herne Bay, but I can arrange to interview your mum in Whitstable if that is more convenient." Ashley didn't care where they met, so long as it happened soon. Eleven o'clock tomorrow felt like an age to wait.

He listened to a brief discussion between Cindy and her mother, fervently hoping Mrs Weaver would once again insist she was fine to receive him now. However, when Cindy next addressed him, it was to confirm she would bring her mother to the nick in

Herne Bay the following morning. She bade him a goodnight, and the conversation concluded.

So far as moving the case alone went, he had struck what felt like gold. Sure, they were barred from investigating Elroy Stewart, but that didn't mean they had to drop the Daniel Mahony case. Ashley thought it possible his boss would hand the case to someone else if Mrs Weaver proved to be good to her word and identified Elroy as the man she saw behind the wheel of the silver BMW, but that was a problem for another day.

Taking a step backwards so she appeared on the other side of the kitchen door, Tanya stepped into sight. She had a glass of wine in her hand - a deep velvety red they both enjoyed, and there was a trace of lipstick on the rim where she had wasted no time taking her first sip. As he always did, Ashley marvelled at how incredibly attractive she was. The dress she wore accentuated her curves in the most sensuous way. He was trim and fit and handsome enough, but if Idris Elba is a ten, Ashley knew he could only scrape a seven and his fiancée was at least two points above him. At least.

Tanya lifted the glass to her lips but paused before taking another sip. "Are you going out?" she asked. "Because if you are not, I could do with a massage."

With a jolt of excitement, for he knew precisely what would happen when the massage concluded, Ashley decided he wasn't quite so upset about not being able to grill Mrs Weaver tonight after all.

Chapter 10

I ARRIVED HOME VIA an off-licence with a bottle of Jameson's Triple Blend Irish whisky under my arm. Mary made a show of tutting and rolling her eyes, but admitted she'd already had two glasses of wine and wasn't surprised to see me coming through the door with my favourite tipple.

We were both under a lot of stress and doing everything we could not to let anyone see it.

I placed the bottle on the kitchen counter and opened my arms as Mary came to give me a hug. We clung to each other, saying nothing until Mary tilted her head back so I could kiss her. Being so short, she had to rise onto her tiptoes and I needed to fold my back, but we have been doing it the same way since we met.

"How did today go?" she asked. "The meeting this morning, I mean. Are you back to working with Ashley again?"

I let my arms fall away as Mary pulled back. I could see she was part way through prepping dinner and wanting to return to the task. From the look of things we were having gammon steaks with homemade chips and fried eggs. My stomach grumbled with interest. Taking a glass from a high cupboard near my head, I picked up the bottle of whisky again.

"The meeting was what I said it would be: a complete waste of time, just like the investigation. That bitch DI Griffiths wasn't happy to let it go. She acts as though I must have orchestrated the attack even if it wasn't me behind the wheel." I poured three fingers into the glass and didn't bother putting the cap back on. "Anyway, it's done now, and I've only got two weeks left."

"And Ashley?"

"Predictably apologetic and embarrassed." I took a healthy glug of the golden liquid, letting it soak into my tastebuds and wash away the day before I swallowed it down. It burned a path through my body, instantly diminishing the anxiety I felt. "We are back to investigating the Bruce Denton case."

Mary, her back to me as she faced the kitchen counter, put down the potato peeler and turned around.

"How worried do I need to be?"

I sighed. I wanted to lie. I could tell her there was nothing to worry about and alleviate her concerns. She wouldn't believe me. Not entirely, but my assurances would help to lessen the fear she held. Selfishly, I wanted someone with whom I could share my own worries, and Mary is the only person on the planet I can talk to about Bruce Denton. If it came down to selfishness, I would have lied to her and said it was all going to be okay, but in the end I knew it was better to be honest with my wife.

"I don't know, darling." I drained my glass, got a disapproving look from Mary and chose to leave refilling it until after we had eaten. "Tomorrow we will start to interview some of the people associated with the case. His neighbours and such. We are going to show them the video and see if doing it face to face jogs anyone's memory."

Colour draining from her face, Mary asked, "Do you think it will?"

All I could do was shrug, but when I spoke I went with an honest answer again.

"I don't think so. The people who remember this case because it touched their lives will have seen the footage. It's been on the news enough times. If they recognised you ... if anyone recognised you, they would have come forward by now. I don't think it will be a problem."

Mary narrowed her eyes a little when she asked, "So why do you look so worried?"

I hate that my wife knows me so well. I can't get away with anything. Even when I act in a manner that would cover up whatever I don't want her to know, she always figures it out anyway.

"Ashley knows that my car was spotted in the street outside Bruce's house." Seeing Mary's mouth drop open in horror, I corrected my statement. "I mean, he knows about the registration, not that the car was mine."

Mary put one hand to her heart. "Oh, thank God. You scared me, Tony. So what does that mean for us?"

"Hopefully nothing. This is where Ashley's keenness finally works in my favour. He's balancing more than one case again, trying to be supercop on his way up the promotion ladder. I pretended I had no idea Vicky's information never made it into the official case file and offered to do the follow up research. It meant he could pursue something juicier, so I did the VRN check, downloaded the results, made sure your old car wasn't listed, and sent him the file. We are safe unless he decides to perform the search again himself."

"You made that sound really simple."

I changed my mind about the whisky but only poured myself a single finger.

"In theory, it is. Like I said, unless Ashley checks my work, which he'll have no reason to do, there will be nothing to find."

"But if the case isn't solved in two weeks when you retire, what will happen to it?"

It was the very question that kept me awake at night and fuelled my need to drink more than I should. For thirty years I've been custodian of the case and could be content no one else would ever look at it. With my retirement, that changed, yet the likelihood of anyone ever picking it up had seemed so remote I've never really given it any thought. Now the situation was very different.

"I have two weeks," I said, trying to reassure myself as much as I was Mary. "That will be enough time to show Ashley there are no leads left to unravel. If the video fails to jog someone's memory and he accepts that the half-promising partial number plate leads nowhere, I think he'll give it up and move onto other cases. He's about results. Besides, I maintain that this whole cold case thing was a political manoeuvre. The chief constable wanted to make it look like he was reacting and now that the focus is no longer on that report, I think the officers involved will be reassigned. They won't waste a lot of time investigating old cases that couldn't be solved the first time."

"But you've already caught two killers who thought they had got away with it."

"That's true, but other than me and Ashley, the teams have yielded no results."

I took another swig of my drink. Mary looked like she had something else to say but she either chose to keep it to herself or dismissed it as unnecessary. Turning back to the kitchen counter, she said, "Dinner will be half an hour or so. Don't have anything else to drink until you've eaten."

Murmuring, "Yes, dear," I kissed the top of her right ear and walked through the house to the office. There I slumped into the battered chair I'd bought second-hand more than twenty years earlier. With half an hour to kill and thoughts of Bruce Denton at the front of my mind, I allowed a flicker of doubt to cloud my thoughts. What if Ashley continued to pursue the case after I retired? It was the wrong question to ask. The right question was what could I do right now to ensure the case was put to bed once and for all?

A voice at the back of my head, one I'd been ignoring since it first chose to voice its opinion, reminded me that I would go to jail for a very long time if Ashley was able to uncover the truth. He was already closer than anyone else had ever come and his determination was such that he'd broken into my desk to retrieve the secret file I kept there. I still didn't know how he found out about its existence and couldn't possibly ask him. Not for the first time, I questioned if I could kill Ashley.

Killing Bruce had been easy, but this would be cold blooded murder. Could I do it? Did I still have the stomach for such a deed? I didn't want to have to find out, and the thought of taking Ashley's life to protect my secret made me sick to my stomach. Yet the alternative was spending the rest of my life in jail.

We were prepared to run if we had to. The port of Dover isn't far away, but disappearing forever isn't an easy thing to do. We would have to ditch the car and buy a new one without leaving a trail that could be followed. Growing more anxious by the second, I needed to distract myself.

With a deep breath to steady myself, I opened my laptop and read over the notes for the Daniel Mahony case. I already knew it all, but anything was better than thinking about Bruce Denton. We needed to find a new angle, a new piece of evidence. Something the original team of investigators failed to find when the case was fresh. It felt improbable.

We had no witnesses. Well, none that were willing to talk.

I stared at the photograph. The one that provided Elroy's alibi. If I accepted that it was staged, then the person wearing Elroy's clothes, his face caught in quarter profile, was someone else. We knew that already, but was there any mileage in figuring out who it could be? I frowned, my eyes moving from one face to the next, noting their expressions, the position of their hands ...

"Who took the photograph?" The question jumped from my brain to my mouth and dived past my lips so fast I didn't have time to consider where it came from.

Someone had to be holding the camera, and I didn't know who that was. Most of Elroy's known associates were in the picture, plus his girlfriend at the time, Helen Hoath-Salter. Scratching at an itch on my chin, I made a note to check in the morning. Maybe the information was there, and I simply hadn't noticed it. Maybe Ashley would know.

Mary called through the house that she was serving dinner. I closed the laptop, determined not to look at it again that night.

Chapter 11

Arriving at work the next morning, I knew I would find Ashley at his desk and figured he'd probably been there for the best part of an hour.

"Coffee?" I asked, placing my bag down and walking around to see what Ashley had on his screen.

Ashley gave a small shake of his head. "Just had one. Are you dying to get some caffeine or can it wait?"

I jinked an eyebrow.

"There was a breakthrough last night," Ashley announced, swivelling his chair to look up at me. He chose to leave it at that, teasing the moment out because it was so juicy.

My heart thumped in my chest. A breakthrough? In which case. To hide my flush of panic, I turned around and crouched to root through my bag.

"Do tell," I encouraged, convinced my voice sounded unnatural. I would never make it as an actor.

"Rachael Weaver is prepared to change her statement."

I snapped my head around to see if Ashley was being serious. Relief flooded through my body, making my head spin. It wasn't anything to do with Bruce Denton. For the last few seconds I had prayed hard that the breakthrough wouldn't be someone coming forward to identify the woman in the video.

"I called her when I got home yesterday afternoon. She has cancer and I got the impression she doesn't have long to live."

"She's clearing her conscience?"

"Something like that. I wanted to get her statement last night, but we missed her yesterday because she was at the hospital having chemotherapy. Her daughter was adamant her mother needed to get some rest, but she is bringing her here this morning. I have reserved an interview room already."

"What time?"

"Eleven."

I considered the news. "This is a breakthrough." Changing the subject slightly, I asked, "Do you know who took the photograph?"

Ashley's eyebrows danced while he attempted to decipher the question. He gave up. "What photograph?"

"THE photograph. The one with Elroy in it even though we are sure he was behind the wheel of the murder weapon."

"Oh, um." Ashley wanted to provide an answer but realised he didn't have one. He scrunched up his face, questioning why he couldn't recall that piece of detail. He prided himself on being the one in the team, whatever team that might be, who knew the case better than anyone else.

I nodded. "I don't know either."

We spent the next ten minutes interrogating the case file until we were forced to accept the answer wasn't there. It made me wonder if no one in 2003 ever thought to ask the question. I couldn't decide whether it would be worth pursuing or would just eat up a bunch of time without delivering anything useful. Ashley seemed happy to let me be the one to pursue it.

On the back of the six-inch by four-inch picture, in a diagonal line, was a printer's mark. It had been made in Boots the Chemist and I could remember when I had used their booths to print holiday snaps. There were some numbers and letters next to the 'Boots' logo but I didn't know what they indicated.

Ashley interrupted my thoughts. "With Mrs Weaver coming in later this morning, I hoped we could get cracking with the list of Bruce Denton's neighbours."

"What? Oh, that's why you asked about needing coffee. If I go without my morning hit of caffeine, we can get around a few of them before Mrs Weaver arrives, right?"

Ashley clapped me on the shoulder. "Good thinking, Tony. I love your initiative."

I thought about kicking him in his bad leg. I didn't need a cup of coffee, but the boost from it wouldn't go amiss. I wasn't sleeping well, even with half a bottle of whisky inside me, but Ashley didn't need to know that.

Ten minutes later I was back behind the wheel of my car and heading for Bruce Denton's house. The sense of dread I felt was tempered by a desire to get it over with. Ever since they dug the damned camcorder out of the bog, going back over my old case with Ashley in tow had been inevitable. Was I ready for it? Heck no, but I never would be. Rather than see myself as about to get caught, I had to flip things around. This was my chance to nail the case shut once and for all. If I got this right, no one would ever look at it again.

At least that's what I kept telling myself on the drive through Herne Bay.

"I got the list of VRNs you sent," Ashley announced out of the blue. "I just realised I haven't replied to your email. But I got it. Is it a long list? I didn't get the chance to open it last night."

"Long enough," I replied. "I think it was more than sixty names in the end. That's what was left after I ruled out women and anyone way outside of the age bracket. It will take hours to go through them all one at a time."

Ashley sucked a little air between his teeth before saying, "But that's what we are going to have to do. It could be the thing that cracks the case."

Not without my name on the list it wouldn't.

"I can do it," I volunteered, sounding unenthusiastic.

"No, I've got it. It's something I can do sitting down."

He wasn't going to be put off and if I pushed again he would question why. Instead of arguing, I said, "It's going to make me look stupid if you manage to find the killer from a partial VRN that was in Vicky's notes the whole time."

There really wasn't anything to say to that and I had just turned into Bruce's street. I parked a couple of doors away from his property and took out my notebook.

"Jamie Porter's parents, Julia and Sam Porter, still live in the same house. Shall we start with them?"

Ashley looked at me. "The parents of the kid who shot the video? Surely they saw the video footage at the time. Weren't they the ones who reported it?"

Ok, he had me there. I knew they wouldn't recognise Mary, but then I was almost certain none of Bruce's neighbours would. There was no reason why they should. Mary only came to the house or the street that one time.

"We can either be thorough or not, Ashley," I replied cooly. "Don't you want to talk to them anyway?"

I scored a point in return, and we went to their door. I knew them to be retired but couldn't be sure they would be home. Julia appeared behind the frosted glass and looked surprised when she saw me on her doorstep. It had been something like five years since we last spoke, and she had aged. Now well into her sixties, she had let her hair go grey, but styled it neatly and kept it short around the back and sides.

"Tony?" she said my name as a question, no doubt wondering why I was back after so much time. It had taken her a second to recall it.

"Mrs Porter, good morning." I introduced Ashley, explained that the case had been reopened, and asked if she had seen the old video footage on the TV, which of course, she had.

"I'm afraid I have no more idea who she is now than I ever did, Tony. Whoever she is, I had never seen her before and I haven't seen her since."

Ashley asked, "Did you often see Bruce with women?"

Julia looked bored by the question. "It was all so long ago. He was just a guy down the street who I saw every now and then if we were both outside at the same time. I'm not sure I even knew his name until someone killed him."

She hadn't. I remembered the first time I interviewed her. It was late evening on the day his body was found and she only knew his name because everyone in the street was talking about him.

A car pulled up outside the house - Sam Porter returning home from wherever he had been.

"Sam was at the doctor's," Julia told us.

We spoke with him briefly, all four of us standing in the cool air. Julia hovered in her doorway, content to leave the door to her little porch open because the one behind it was closed. They didn't know anything and that proved to be the trend for the morning. There were six of Bruce's neighbours still living in the street and none of them had any idea who the woman in the video could be.

The one neighbour who remembered Bruce more vividly than the others was Rose Shaw. She lived opposite his house and would have seen him coming and going more easily than anyone else. Rose also knew him because she was one his teachers when he was at junior school. Bruce kept mostly to himself, but he interacted with Rose, chatting in the street when they bumped into each other. She had told me about the string of women he brought to the house. It was clear she didn't approve, not that she expressed it in words, but even she didn't recognise Mary from the video.

Ashley played it for her on a tablet with a large screen.

There were other names on the list – neighbours who had moved away and former colleagues and friends who could, tangibly, have known Bruce well enough to have met a woman he was dating. But he wasn't dating her. He met her that day. Obviously, I couldn't tell Ashley that and why would I want to? He could waste as much of my time as he wanted. The more people he spoke to, the more clearly he would understand that this case couldn't be solved.

Not unless he decided to redo the search of the partial VRN.

At ten thirty, we headed back to the station. Mrs Weaver was going to be there soon.

Chapter 12

I HALF EXPECTED MRS Weaver to be at the nick waiting for us. Ashley had made it sound like she was keen to get the truth off her chest, but waltzing back through the station door at quarter to eleven, they were yet to arrive.

I made coffee, offered Ashley one, which he again declined, and got back to the office to find him rereading the statement she gave in 2003. Rachael came forward when a request was made for information regarding a speeding silver BMW. The report on the local news showed the car at the time – a CCTV camera caught it leaving the vicinity of the murder at speed – but the footage was too grainy for the driver to be identified.

Rachael remembered the car because the driver screeched to a stop at a junction to avoid an accident and then burned rubber, quite literally, when it pulled away again. At the time, Rachael was walking her dog, a Westy, and approaching the corner. The driver looked right at her when he turned his head to check the road was clear. She estimated the distance between them at less than ten feet and identified Elroy Stewart as the driver just two days later. She specifically remembered his gold tooth and when called to view an identity parade, had the six young men bare their teeth.

Less than a week after that she retracted her statement, just like Christine Westbury. They both claimed to have been mistaken. Yes, the man they saw was black, but it wasn't Elroy. Their reports differed at that point, Christine stating that the man she saw was older and had greying hair. Rachael's revised statement claimed confusion. She hadn't really seen the man at all, only getting a vague impression of his face when his car sped by.

The transcript of the interview, conducted by none other than my superintendent back when he was just a sergeant, left no doubt she wasn't believed. He even asked if she had been threatened, to which she also lied.

The sudden reversal now, if that was what we were about to get, whether due to her failing health or some other motivation, was a gift. Solving the case would make Ashley look great, would annoy Superintendent Charters no end, which was fun for me, and score yet another victory for the cold case team. But would it make Ashley look for a next case so he could continue his winning streak, or convince him to double down on Bruce Denton?

I had no idea.

At 1102hrs I found myself looking out of the window. I expected the old girl to be on time. The interview room was set up and waiting. All we needed was the lady in question to keep her appointment.

By 1113hrs I questioned if Ashley had the time right? Or the day.

"Yes," he replied with a discontented frown and a glance at his watch. "Eleven today. Mrs Weaver's daughter was quite clear."

"They could be running late for a dozen different reasons."

I'm sure Ashley knew that too, but his driven nature wouldn't allow him to just sit around patiently.

"I'm calling the daughter," he said.

I looked out the window again, watching the cars coming down the street to see if one would turn into the carpark.

Behind me, Ashley said, "No answer." When I looked over my shoulder, he had the phone back to his ear. "House phone," he mouthed, his expression changing abruptly when the line connected. Instantly smiling as he switched to engaging and pleasant, his bright demeanour didn't last.

I only got his half of the conversation, but his face told me enough.

He ended the call with, "We are leaving now," and aimed his eyes at me. "Mrs Weaver died during the night. It looks like she fell down the stairs."

I bit my lip, debating whether to speak the words that had jumped into my mouth.

But I didn't need to. When my eyes locked on Ashley's, he said, "Or she was pushed."

Chapter 13

FILLED WITH DISAPPOINTMENT, FRUSTRATION, and definitely battling some anger, we raced to Whitstable. Had Elroy killed her because she was going to talk? Had he sent a minion? How had he found out? Or were we drawing false conclusions? For Elroy to be able to react so fast he would have to be listening to Rachael's conversations.

Ashley discussed the historic crime with Mrs Weaver over the phone less than twenty-four hours ago. Now she was dead. It suggested he had the place bugged and a person constantly listening. Neither of us believed that would be true.

So what then?

Electing to end the speculation until we knew more, we rode the final mile in silence. When he called the house, Ashley had spoken to a cop, a young man from the Whitstable nick. He'd been dispatched along with a colleague when Cindy found her mum in a twisted heap at the bottom of the stairs.

Ashley had told him the old lady was an active witness in an ongoing murder investigation and made it very clear he was to keep the house secure. If she had been pushed, there would be evidence. Criminals always leave behind far more than they think.

Well, except in my case.

I parked my old blue Astra behind the squad car and hurried to the house with Ashley following in my wake.

The PC must have seen us coming because the door opened before we could get to it.

"DS Long?" he enquired, looking at me.

I aimed a thumb over my head. "That's him. I'm DS Tony Heaton. Who's inside?"

"My colleague and the old lady's daughter. The doctor got here before me and has already confirmed death. He had the team from the funeral director on their way, but I delayed them."

His tone wanted me to confirm he'd done the right thing, which he had.

"What's your colleague's name?"

"Debbie. Debs. She in there with the daughter, drinking tea and chatting. The daughter seems to be taking it well enough."

We were talking in hushed tones, making sure our voices wouldn't carry inside the house.

"Has she said anything about the timing of her mother's fall?"

He flicked his eyes to Ashley. "Not so far."

I started forward, moving the kid back and out of my way by invading his personal space. The door opened into a hallway so narrow the PC had to flatten himself against the wall. Old houses are built that way. A door to our right took us into the small living room where we found Cindy sitting on her mum's sofa next to a young woman in uniform. They both looked up.

Debs made to get up, reacting as though we had caught her skiving because she was having a cup of tea with a recently bereaved person. I waved for her to stay where she was.

"Cindy," I crossed the room to sit in an armchair set adjacent to the sofa. "I'm so sorry for your loss. Was it you who found her?" I had a whole bunch of difficult questions to ask her and needed to ease her in gently.

Cindy had been crying; the standard reaction that follows the shock of realising a person is really gone. Her eyes were still puffy, but she was past that stage now and likely making a mental list of all the people she needed to tell and all the things she now had to do.

Cindy nodded rather than speak her reply. It made me wonder if she didn't yet trust her voice not to crack, but she did have something to say.

"She was at the bottom of the stairs. I wanted to get one of those stair lift things fitted. She would have qualified for one through the NHS, but she always said she would rather move her bed into one of the downstairs rooms than admit she was that frail." Cindy's hands were wrapped around a teacup and resting in her lap. She was looking down at them, her focus nowhere except when she lifted her eyes occasionally to look at me.

"Has she been moved?" I asked, instantly wincing. I should have waited before pushing forward. I was about to introduce the idea that she might have been pushed and was being clumsy about it.

Cindy looked up again. "Moved? The doctor checked her when he got here, but I knew she was gone the moment I saw her. I checked her pulse and tried to shut her eyes, but they wouldn't close. They always close people's eyes on TV." She was rambling a little, which was entirely in keeping with my experience of relatives at this stage of their grief, but had answered the question.

"You came in through the front door?" I sought to confirm.

Cindy looked up at me again, confusion in her eyes. "Yes." Why was I asking questions about the house.

I heard rather than saw Ashley leave the room. He was going to check the back door.

"Did your mum leave a key outside in case she ever locked herself out?"

Her frown deepened, but Cindy said, "Yes. It's under one of those fake rock things in the back garden. Why ..." With a gasp, she glimpsed where my questions were heading. "You think this is because she was going to talk to you about that murder!"

Remaining calm as I faced her growing hysteria, I said, "I need to rule it out. I will have officers here soon to check the property and look for evidence." We were yet to set that in motion, but it would only take a call. They were going to have to dust for prints, check for signs of forced entry, look for footprints in the carpet pile ... I confirmed Cindy was yet to go upstairs, and asked the two PCs already at the scene to keep her in the living room. She would be fine there for now, but once her statement had been taken, it would be necessary to remove her from the property. At least until the forensics team was finished.

I still doubted her house was bugged, but the timeliness of Mrs Weaver's death demanded a check be conducted.

I thought Cindy might shout and get angry, but she went the other way, pulling her feet up under her body to make herself smaller. It was a defensive measure to keep the world at bay. Leaving her to silently reflect, I found Ashley in the kitchen.

"Back door was locked, but I heard Mrs Gunderson say there is a key. When will people learn not to do that?"

"Probably never." Like every other police officer, it pained me that people make it so easy for the criminals to gain entry to their houses. The fake rocks were the worst because they were like a flashing beacon to announce the location of the key.

Taking a walk around the house, rather than put my fingerprints on the handle to the back door, I looked about. I needed less than ten seconds to locate the fake rock, but I didn't lift it to look for the key. Maybe there wouldn't be any prints on the plastic object, but I wasn't about to obliterate them if there were.

Crouching, I examined it, and a couple of nearby flowerpots for signs they had been moved, but there was no telltale ring of dirt to show they had been lifted in the recent past.

"Everything all right?" asked a voice from my right. It caught me by surprise, but not enough to make me jump.

It was the neighbour again. The man by himself this time. He was looking over the garden fence which was five feet tall and then had a trellis portion on top so he was looking through it more than over it.

Coming out of my crouch, I addressed him. "No, sir, I'm afraid not. It is my sad duty to inform you that your neighbour passed away during the night." I hadn't planned to start the process of speaking with the neighbours until after we had reason to believe her fall was no accident, but here I was. "Did you hear or see anything last night?"

The question surprised him, and I think he was about to ask what I meant when his wife came out of their back door.

"Rachael's dead!" he blurted.

"Dead?"

"Yes! Dead!"

I wanted them to lower their voices, but they did so before I had to say anything. He went to her, wrapping his arms around her for comfort and I had to stand quietly while they held each other tightly.

When they broke apart, the man's hand finding his wife's, he said, "Was she murdered?"

It was my turn to be caught by surprise. I couldn't deny the possibility, but I guess my face questioned how he'd made the leap because he said, "You asked if I saw or heard anything last night. You're hoping I might have seen the killer."

I raised my hands, palms down to make 'slow down' gestures.

"There is an enquiry whenever a person dies unexpectedly." I chose not to say that it was usually conducted by the coroner. "My questions were just routine. In all likelihood, your neighbour died of natural causes. So did you?"

"Hear anything last night?" The man repeated my question and checked with his wife before shaking his head. "No, I'm afraid not. What time would it have been?"

That was another thing for the coroner to figure out.

They didn't know anything, and from the look of things, if Rachael's death was murder, her killer didn't need to use her key to get in.

Chapter 14

THE FORENSICS TEAM CAME and went, the process of checking over the house taking less time than it would for an obvious murder yet still eating up the rest of the day. The sun descended, shadows outside lengthening then merging until the streetlights came on to create new ones.

The coroner's estimate for time of death was around midnight. There were skin cells from her right knee on the wall halfway down the stairs and a matching scratch where her flesh met with the rough Artex surface. Small flecks of paint and plaster from the Artex were embedded in her skin.

It was enough to convince me she had fallen down the stairs and not simply been arranged there to make it look like a fall. That didn't mean she hadn't been pushed, but by quarter to five when I ought to have been starting to pack my bag and think about heading home, the forensic team was yet to find anything that would suggest foul play.

There were some fingerprints that matched neither the home-owner's nor her daughter's, but I wasn't expecting to find them in the database. They could be from a repairman or a relative who came to visit. We would be thorough, but as the day wore on, I became more and more convinced we were wasting our time. Rachael Weaver was supposed to give us the lead we needed to make something out of the case. Her death stopped her from spilling the proverbial beans and we were right back where we started.

Nowhere.

Evidence proving she had been murdered would take us in a whole new direction that might eventually lead us back to Daniel Mahony's killer, but either the killer was really careful or poor old Rachael simply fell. I would wait for the full report, but I wasn't going to hold my breath.

With the forensics team packing up, I was acutely aware that my day had gone sideways. The plan, ha ha, (like such a thing exists) had been to grind Ashley down on the Bruce Denton case, but other than the first couple of hours this morning, we hadn't looked at it. I wanted to rejoice that he'd not been able to go through the list of VRNs, but I knew we were only putting that off. The sooner he tackled it, the sooner he would accept it was another dead end.

I would try again tomorrow, and held a little more hope that I would succeed because Elroy Stewart and the Daniel Mahony enquiry had never looked more out of reach.

When my phone rang, I expected to see Mary's name on the screen. She would be calling to ask what time I would be home so she could get on with dinner. But it wasn't Mary. It was just a number.

"Detective Sergeant Heaton," I answered.

"This is ..." a timid voice said. "This is ... it's Emily. Emily Harris."

My head shot up, looking for Ashley. I was in the kitchen, snaffling chocolate digestives and drinking tea. My partner was elsewhere, actually doing his job and getting involved. I went looking for him.

"Yes, Emily. Thank you for calling. What can I do for you? Are you okay?" When I handed her my card I never once thought she would call it.

"Um." She sounded nervous. "Look, can we meet? I need to tell you something about why I said the things I said."

"I'm listening."

"Not over the phone," she replied, her voice quiet and filled with trepidation. "I'm at work. Can you come to me?"

It served as a perfect demonstration of my change in attitude over the last few weeks that I didn't immediately think of who I could send in my place. Prior to the cold case taskforce and working with Ashley, you were lucky to still find me in work at this time.

"Give me the address." I had made my way through the house to arrive outside the front door where Ashley was talking to the head of the forensic team. Tapping his shoulder, I showed him that I was on a call, and with my hand over the phone, I said, "It's Emily Harris. She wants to meet."

That got his attention.

Meanwhile, Emily was being a flustered mess. She had started giving me the name of the place where she was working but stopped to admit she was working off the books. When I first looked into her, the lack of job made me suspicious. For some it's an indication of criminal activity – they have money coming in but not from a source they wish to declare. For most others, they don't want to share what they earn with the tax man, so they hide their employment and take cash in hand.

Emily fell into the latter category. Probably. The nature of her involvement with Elroy was yet to be determined. Either way, she thought telling me where she worked was going to ruin it and getting caught dodging tax by His Majesty's Revenue and Customs comes with severe implications.

"Emily, I think that's the last thing you should be worried about, but trust me, I am not obligated to report your employment. It will stay between us. Okay."

She needed a little more encouragement, but eventually she gave me the address. She was working as a cleaner at an electrical wholesaler's outlet called Ellison's Electricals, on an industrial estate in Tankerton. It was just a few miles away. I had the name of the business and her advice that the place would be closed by the time she got there. She didn't want to get caught on the CCTV camera that covered the loading yard of the businesses in the estate but assured me the back door would be left unlocked and ajar so I would know which one I wanted.

I relayed all this to Ashley when our call ended. I had promised to be there within thirty minutes.

"She gave you no indication what she wants to tell us?" he asked.

I gave a one shoulder shrug. "Nope. She was tight-lipped on the subject, but look, it's got to be Elroy, hasn't it? She's scared and has come to realise there is only one way to get out from under his thumb."

Ashley muttered, "Let's hope that's the case," and turned back to the guy from forensics. They were done and the house was ready to be locked up. Cindy had long since gone home where I would guess she was drinking something alcoholic and making phone calls. As Rachael's only child there would be much for her to do in the coming days.

I would take the set of house keys she left with me to Cindy's house in the morning. For now, I locked up, checked the back door and all the windows were closed, and joined Ashley at my car.

My stomach rumbled its emptiness, but it was going to have to wait. Once again, there was a chance we could find a way to get at Elroy Stewart.

Chapter 15

PLOUGH LANE INDUSTRIAL ESTATE is a rather grand title for the small line of budget enterprises it housed, and it sat all the way over on the other side of Tankerton. While technically still in Whitstable, and closer to the suburb of Swalecliffe, it's only locals like me who still count it as part of Tankerton.

Regardless, getting there meant taking the old Herne Bay Road through rush hour traffic and I worried my promise to be there in under thirty would prove to be a lie. If we had been in Ashley's Mondeo I could have switched on the lights and sirens.

My car was fitted with them too, but when Ashley suggested we could move faster by forcing the traffic ahead to get out of our way, I had to admit the system didn't work.

"Really?" he questioned. "Can't they fix it?"

"Not without me reporting that it's broken I suspect."

Ashley rolled his eyes. "How long ago did it break?"

I sucked on my lips, feigning deep thought before saying, "What year is it now?" The truth was that it packed in so long ago I couldn't remember when it last worked but had used it so rarely it could have stopped working years before I discovered it was faulty.

We crawled through the streets, bumper to bumper with the other drivers, conscious of the time ticking by. It wasn't so much the case that there were too many cars, just too many for the old seaside resort's tiny roads. Twice a day, nay three times if one includes the mid-afternoon crush of mums collecting the kids from school, the central arteries running through the town clog. It doesn't last long and it's caused more by workers coming home from jobs elsewhere than it is workers in the town leaving to go home. Whitstable is not a hub of business activity. There are no high-rise office blocks, and no multinational firms are looking to site their British HQ there. Even though the views would be nice and the air is pleasant.

The clock in my head clicked past the thirty-minute mark just before we made the final turn and I hoped Emily had been watching the clock and getting more nervous. I wanted her on edge and scared. It was time to undo what she did by revealing the truth and admitting you have lied isn't a task one undertakes while feeling refreshed and relaxed.

True to her word, the back door was ajar. Set into a wall without windows, a sign above the steel door requested all visitors report to the office at the front with an arrow pointing around the building. It was just one unit in a row of half a dozen. Another half a dozen faced it and ten of the twelve appeared to be operating. One sold tyres, two were knocked together to provide a mechanic's place. Another was a company that made golf bags.

I parked with Ashley nearest to the door, so he got to it before me. Opening it up, he looked inside. A corridor led deeper into the building. There were old newspapers stacked up on both sides, but set a few feet apart so it was like a chicane to get in. Weaving between them, I questioned what they were doing there and mentally remarked about the fire hazard they represented.

"Emily Harris?" he called. His voice echoed slightly, reverberating off the roof high above our heads. The corridor was built of brick but had no ceiling. It ran along the dividing wall between this unit and the next one. That was on our right. Behind the wall to our left would be offices and storerooms. At the front we would find the customer area of the shop with a counter and shelves of goods arranged to look attractive and make the visitors decide to just 'grab that while I'm here'.

Emily didn't answer, but the lights were on and I could imagine her polishing or mopping with a set of earbuds keeping the outside world at bay.

I called her name as I ventured along the corridor. She would be here somewhere, bevering away to earn a wage she would never declare.

"Emily?" I called her name again. I had reached the end of the corridor and was coming into the hub of the operation. I could see the front counter and if I turned my head the empty offices were behind me. A vacuum cleaner sat in the middle of the floor, its lead snaking away to a socket in the wall opposite me.

I could see the whole of the building, and Emily wasn't here. Unless she was in the restroom cleaning that. That had to be what it was.

Except it wasn't.

The whump of ignition from behind me was matched by another a half second later when flames shot up inside the closed entrance door.

Ashley swore and hobble-ran to the exit. Not that he could get to it. Flames were coming under the door, courtesy of whatever liquid accelerant was being used. The smell of it reached my nose, and the smoke the fire produced began to tickle my throat.

Suddenly the newspapers made sense. They weren't there by accident. Both stacks, each roughly three feet high, were on fire.

Through the letterbox at the front of the unit, an unseen hand posted a Molotov cocktail. It wasn't a big one. In fact, if my eyes hadn't deceived me the bottle of choice once held Miller Lite, but either way it hit the floor and smashed, adding to the flames already licking at a display of work clothes.

With both exits now blocked by flame, I found myself immobile. I knew I ought to be doing something but couldn't quite work out what that should be.

Ashley ripped his jacket off and used it to beat at the flames by the back door. The low pile carpet there was ablaze. Down in a crouch, and with his broken arm up to protect his face from the heat, he ignored his injuries and fought the fire.

I swung my head to look at the front door. There ought to be fire extinguishers visible. Every business is subject to the same scrutiny and checks so it wasn't as though they could decide not to bother. The unit, maybe twelve yards from the front wall to the back one, didn't need long to fill with smoke. It clawed at my throat and seared my eyes. I coughed, my chest spasming as I rallied my brain.

Looking for the distinct red that would indicate where the fire extinguishers were located, I found it, but the station was empty. Not so much as a fire blanket had been left for us. It was a trap, and we had walked right into it like willing fools.

I couldn't stop coughing. Each attempt at a breath served as a reminder that we were truly screwed. The exits were blocked by flame. At the front of the shop the fire was spreading. Just five or so seconds had elapsed since the fire started and the display stand of clothes next to the door was an inferno. Flames licked upward, heading for the ceiling tiles, and they spread across the floor toward us. There was no chance we could get out that way.

The rear exit was worse, the newspapers were a towering inferno and because the corridor had no ceiling, the flames roared into the air high above our heads. There was nothing up there for them to catch and the newspapers would burn themselves out soon enough. Not before we asphyxiated to death, though.

Weirdly, I wasn't as panicked as I knew I should have been. I was moments from death, unable to breathe, and so hot I expected to look down and find my clothing on fire. Yet, I felt strangely calm. It was almost as though it was happening to someone else and I was watching it on TV. In the next few moments, I would lose consciousness and there would be no more dire dread about Bruce Denton. Ashley would die next to me, and the case would forever remain unsolved. Mary, my dear Mary, would be free to live the rest of her life without the danger of discovery hanging over her head.

Of course, she would have to do it without me which would make her life completely pointless ...

Staring at Ashley, as he valiantly fought against the burning newspapers blocking our exit, I saw that I had another way out of my dilemma. All I had to do was give him a shove. The fire was so hot it kept pushing him back. Kind of in a standing crouch, he would dart forward to swat at the flames with his jacket, but that was already on fire. If I timed it right, I could barrel him into the midst of the fire, and I would never see him again. No one could survive more than half a second of that heat.

From some fire safety training I had been subjected to goodness knows when in the past, I knew most people in fires die because they breath in the superheated air and fry their lungs. That was going to happen to us soon and I recalculated to see whether I thought I could use Ashley to create a bridge to the exit. If he knocked over one of the newspaper towers ...

A twanging noise from above out heads made me look up. One of the light fittings had come loose, but only from one end. It swung from the end still connected, prescribing an arc through the air. I was hunkered over already, getting my head and everything else closer to the ground as the smoke continued to fill the air. Seeing the six-foot long fitting swinging toward me, I dropped, but I needn't have worried. It was never going to hit me.

It was always going to hit Ashley first. Dangly from two thin steel cables, it hit him square in the head, bowling him backward to land flat on his back next to me. He groaned once and laid still.

My dual plan to murder him to solve my Bruce Denton problem and escape by sacrificing him both went out the window.

Window.

I swung my head around to look at the front of the unit. It was all glass with a display inside. For a brief moment my hope lifted, but the very nature of an industrial unit dictated the front window and door were covered by a steel mesh screen that rolled down to be secured into the ground outside during non-business hours. I could see it beyond the glass even through the roiling black smoke. I could probably find something to break the glass but there was no getting out even if I did.

As if to highlight my plight, the front window chose that moment to smash all by itself. The display in the window had gone up, a mannequin wearing workman's clothes, a cardboard cutout displaying tools in the hands of an attractive woman wearing inappropriate clothing for the task at hand, plus whatever else was there had combined to heat the glass beyond breaking point.

Air blew in, clearing the smoke but at the same time bringing fresh fuel for the flames. I would run out of air in the next few seconds. That was if the heat didn't kill me first.

"Hey! Anyone in there?" A voice cut through the roar of the flames and I swear cold water splashed on me.

Unable to believe my luck, I shouted, "Over here!" Doing so brought on a fresh bout of coughing, my chest heaving as I tried to get air into my lungs.

Mercifully, the voice shouted a reply. "Stay there! We're coming to you!"

I got about a nanosecond to analyse the message before a jet of water soaked me. Sound bombarded me. The flames were loud, but cutting over their din came a rending metal noise. Water pummelled me, stealing away the overwhelming and inescapable heat. It came with such power it pushed me back into the wall.

Two seconds ago I couldn't breathe because there was no air. Now each breath I snatched came with a pint of water and I choked and coughed just as hard as I had before.

Shouts filled the air, vibrations in the floor telling me people were coming. Bewildered, I looked up to find dark shadows blocking out the light coming through the ruined front façade. Hands gripped me and I was hoisted from the floor.

"My partner!" I shouted. The jet of freezing cold water had pushed me away from him. If I hadn't pointed, they might not have noticed his crumpled form. Fighting against the hands that wanted to help me, I threw myself back to the floor to find his body.

Instinct, or whatever you want to call it, demanded I get him to safety. All thoughts of ending his suspicions were gone. I had to save him.

"Let us!" bellowed a voice by my ear. It came through a mask that made it sound like the person was speaking from inside a box, but the next thing I knew a second mask was pressed against my face.

I was being pulled away, but when I turned to look, two fire-fighters were lifting Ashley from the puddle of water. Dragged bodily through the wall of sound, the debris of the unit, the retreating flames, and ever-present smoke, I was lifted up and over the display in the front window to land on the cold ground outside.

Chill wind bit at my exposed skin, the November temperature exacerbated by the water soaking my body and clothes.

"Are you burned?" an urgent voice demanded. There was a light in my face and a pair of eyes behind it.

I managed to wheeze, "No," before a fresh coughing bout seized me.

"Police," I heard Ashley say. "We're police." He was in no better shape than me, but he was conscious again and talking.

My senses returning, I took in the fire engine and firefighters. How they had arrived so quickly I could not fathom, but our escape came courtesy of their swift reactions. Glancing back at the wholesale shop, the flames were gone. Steam rose, filling the air as it fled the shop window. The steel shutter was hanging half off, a cable from the fire engine's winch responsible for ripping it free of its mounts.

"Tony?" coughed Ashley. "You okay?"

I lifted my left arm, giving him a thumbs up instead of attempting to reply. Doing so would surely have brought on yet another coughing fit.

The lights atop the fire engine rotated slowly, filling the darkness with dancing light. I shivered, but as I recovered both physically and mentally, my anger took over. Emily Harris led us into a trap so we could be killed. I wasn't in any state to carry out an arrest, but I was going to do it anyway. She wasn't acting alone. In fact, it was possible she was never at the industrial unit, but there had been people front and back at the same time, coordinating the attack so both our exits were blocked. We were lucky to be alive and now it was time to make someone pay.

I took out my radio. Water ran out of it when I held it aloft. My phone next, but it was equally as dead.

"Mine too," croaked Ashley.

Chapter 16

"Whoa! Where do you think you're going?" A firefighter touched my arm when I levered myself off the ground. They had provided blankets and were waiting on an ambulance to arrive.

I gently moved his hand away. "I need to report this and the people behind it could be getting away. They will think we are dead."

As though voicing his agreement, Ashley also shrugged off his blankets and stood up. He looked half frozen, which was exactly how I felt, but surviving the attack gave us a big advantage. This time Emily would have no defence, and she would be forced to give up Elroy and whoever else was involved or face the crime herself.

"Then call it in," said the firefighter.

"What's going on?" asked another of his team, this one a tall woman with striking red hair.

"They want to go after the people who trapped them in there," the first guy reported.

"Are you guys crazy?" the woman asked. "You need to get checked out at the hospital."

I was about to argue when I started coughing again. I knew they were right; I had inhaled a whole lungful of acrid smoke. Ashley had too, but apart from the coughing, the bruises from being hit with a water cannon, the cold that was beginning to penetrate down to my bones, and the fact that I was utterly soaked, I felt fine. Ashley had a lump on the left side of his forehead where the light unit hit him, but it wasn't life-threatening, and he didn't appear to be concussed.

An ambulance rounded the corner, moving swiftly as it entered the industrial unit. The strobing light from the fire engine illuminated the paramedics inside.

The male firefighter waved them over, walking away from me and Ashley as though the matter was settled.

"I need a phone," I stated bluntly. This was a law enforcement matter, and I would take a phone if I had to.

The redhead offered me hers and I called the nick in Herne Bay.

PC Stacey Dean answered, and I talked right over the top of her to get my message across. Meanwhile the paramedics joined us and started fussing. They wanted me to end the call and, fair enough, I was coughing half the time, but I needed Stacey to mobilise people. She was sending uniforms directly to Emily's address. They would arrest her on sight, and if she wasn't at home, they would start the search to find her.

Only once I was sure things were in motion did I hand back the redhead's phone.

"What's his temperature?" asked one of the paramedics.

They were both in their forties, and both women. They were of stout build and devoid of makeup. One had long brown hair pinned up onto her head. The other's hair was buzzed short on the right side but hung to her jawline around the rest of her scalp.

It was the longer haired woman who posed the question. The one with the short hair aimed a gun-looking device at my head. It beeped a second later.

"Hypothermic," she declared.

Standing a foot or so behind her, the redhead had the blankets again.

"We need to get you both warm and you need to be checked for smoke inhalation," said the paramedic with the long hair. Perhaps sensing my intention to argue, she added, "Smoke inhalation is no joke, gentlemen. The effects can be long lasting and quite terrible. We're talking chronic obstructive pulmonary disease, an increase in the likelihood of heart attacks and strokes, it can impair your cognitive function," she switched her gaze to Ashley, "it can cause impotence ..."

"Maybe we should get checked out," said Ashley.

"Not to mention that you are both going to pass out from hypothermia if you don't get out of those wet clothes and warm up," added her colleague.

They were tag teaming us, and they were right, even though I didn't want them to be. I really could feel the cold seeping into my bones and much as I wanted to voice an argument, it was all I could do to not cough.

Reluctantly, I accepted defeat and wondered how long this would take. The uniforms would be knocking on Emily's door any minute. All they had to go on was my report, given verbally. It was enough, but I wanted to get to her and conduct my interview before she had a chance to dream up some story that would clear her name. She was our link to Elroy and the rest of his criminal buddies. I wanted to get them all now. Not later.

With the paramedics leading us, and the firefighters following to make sure we didn't collapse covering the eight yards to the ambulance, a question occurred to me.

Twisting slightly so I could make eye contact, I asked, "Say, how did you get to us so quickly?"

The redhead was nearest, and she answered, "There was an anonymous tip off. We expected it to be a hoax, but we have to go anyway. Good thing too, really."

Yeah, good thing too. But who provided the tip off?

Chapter 17

The ambulance delivered us to Canterbury Accident and Emergency where we were received by the usual hurried, but far from panicked, medical professionals one always finds waiting. I'm sure the doctors and nurses have that gear within themselves but reserve it for when it is truly needed.

Encouraged to strip out of our wet clothing, we were given base layers and dressing gowns to don and help doing it because our fingers were numb. I baulked at stripping off my underpants, but the nurses – two men – were quite insistent. Ashley didn't seem to care about anything other than getting warm. Or perhaps he was happy to take it all off because he's still in his twenties and goes to the gym. A lot, by the look of things.

The warm clothing took care of the hypothermia, which I think they were exaggerating anyway. The bigger concern was the smoke in our lungs, so we were taken to a room where we received what the doctors called oxygen therapy. Basically, we had masks supplying oxygen. It was supposed to reverse oxygen deprivation.

We were to be monitored to make sure no delayed symptoms arose, but they didn't specify what those might be. They brought me a landline so I could call Mary, but I told her to stay at home because I would be undergoing treatment for hours and I was in no danger.

Then I called the nick and finally got an update on Emily Harris. I had hoped they might find a way to get the information to me, but accepted that with no phone or radio, I was difficult to reach.

The news didn't take long to relay. She was gone.

Ashley had some minor burns to his left arm where he tried to fight the fire at the back door, but otherwise he was about the same as me.

When I told him the uniforms hadn't been able to arrest Emily, he asked, "They have the ports being monitored, right?"

"Yes." It's standard practice for the Kent police to send the port authority details of any criminals deemed likely to flee. It's standard practice, but it rarely works. If they were going to flee, a person can get there fast enough that they will be out of the country before we can catch on. I could only recall one time when a successful arrest was made, and it was the French cops that got the perp when he drove off the train in Calais. It was the chief reason Mary and I were planning to go if we truly believed we were about to be caught.

With the Herne Bay cops out looking for Emily Harris, there really wasn't anything we could do. Had they arrested her, I would be itching to get to the nick so I could conduct the interview. Instead, I laid back my head and closed my eyes.

I guess I dozed off because I came to with voices in the room. Eyelids fluttering, I saw DCI Harris talking to Ashley. Superintendent Charters was with him. They were both dressed casually; pulled from their homes by the news of their stricken officers. It was the second time my boss had come to visit me in the hospital in a month. It was also the second time any boss I had ever endured had come to see me in the hospital. How was it that I was dicing with death so frequently right at the end of my career?

Ashley dipped his head in my direction, drawing the attention of the two senior officers.

"Ah, Tony," Superintendent Charters addressed me as if we were pals. "How are you feeling?"

I shuffled backward a little so I could sit up in bed. I have always hated being visited in hospital. The first time it happened was when I was six or seven years old and suffering from diabolical constipation. I was in my pyjamas and everyone else was dressed. It made me feel weird and uncomfortable then and nothing had changed.

"I'm fine, thank you, sir. I believe this," I wafted my hand at the oxygen bottle and the mask on my face, "is merely precautionary."

His expression, never far from dour, delved a little deeper into the emotional box to achieve grumpy. "Well, mind you don't make any attempt to discharge yourself before the doctors give you the all-clear."

I didn't bother to respond.

"Is that clear, Heaton?"

And there it was. I was Tony for less than a minute. He didn't care about my health. I was to stay in the hospital because further health complications would cause him paperwork.

Unwilling to release his gaze, there was no inflection in my tone when I said, "Perfectly."

Satisfied, with that part at least, he changed the subject. "I'm given to understand you are still pursuing the Daniel Mahony enquiry after you were expressly instructed not to do so."

I had a retort loaded, but it was DCI Harris who got in first.

"Actually, sir, the instruction was to stay away from Elroy Stewart, the chief suspect in the Daniel Mahony case."

"And how is that any different?" Charters demanded, his eyes never leaving mine.

I let a smile tease my mouth. "Because we obeyed the instruction, sir. We were happily conducting enquiries into the murder of Bruce Denton when we stumbled upon a fresh lead that may have brought into question Mr Stewart's alibi. Unfortunately, the witness in question died during the night."

The jolt of surprise on the superintendent's face brought me immense joy. He was always a lousy cop, and I love how out of touch he is with the investigations going on under his nose.

"She fell down the stairs, sir, though it's possible she was pushed. I had the forensic team out this morning, sir. I'm surprised you were not aware."

A muscle spasmed in his jaw as he bit his anger down. I was goading him.

"Regardless," I continued, "our efforts were focused on Bruce Denton when the call from Emily Harris came in. She lied to create the legal barrier that now exists between us and Elroy

Stewart. She made it sound like she was ready to change her story ..."

"So you thought you would let her lead you to an industrial unit tucked out of the way where you could be locked inside and burned alive."

I continued to smile brightly. "That's it, sir." Moron.

Again it was DCI Harris who intervened. "Had she withdrawn her story, it would have exposed that Elroy Stewart lied and provided us with cause to question him as to why."

The superintendent knew that, of course. He's not completely stupid, but it did mess with his desire to make everything my fault.

We were treading on thin ice in continuing to pursue the Daniel Mahony murder, but so long as we didn't go after Elroy and skirted around the side, there really wasn't anything anyone could do to stop us. Or so I thought.

Turning to face DCI Harris, my boss said, "I want them off the case."

DCI Harris didn't try to hide his surprise. "Sir?"

"I'm not having this blow up on my turf. Elroy Stewart's lawyers are just waiting for an excuse to come after us. They get one sniff that these two," he hooked a thumb in my direction, "are still trying to pin a murder on him, and I'll get an unpleasant call from the chief constable."

"But from my understanding he's almost certainly guilty of murder, sir. That was the whole point of the cold case taskforce. They have already solved two historic crimes, sir."

"Yes, well, be that as it may, I was on the original team investigating the murder twenty years ago. He had ironclad alibis back then and still has now. That's right, isn't it, Heaton?" This time he didn't bother to look my way when he addressed me.

"No, sir."

My boss, DCI Harris, and Ashley all snapped their heads around to look at me.

"He has flimsy alibis that are coming apart at the seams. He's frightened. He knows we are closing in and tonight's little adventure showed just how scared he is. Had Mrs Weaver not fallen down the stairs, which I'm still not convinced was an accident, we would be halfway to proving his guilt. His defence relies on a house of cards that is already wobbling." I spoke with my usual confidence, even though I didn't really say anything of worth.

"Off the case," Superintendent Charters growled. "Effective immediately."

DCI Harris attempted to object. "Sir ..."

Looking at me, Charters held up a hand to block DCI Harris's face. "There are plenty of other cases they can pursue, are there not?" He spoke with a gruff tone that threatened increasing volume if anyone was dumb enough to argue.

I was used to it and felt more than ready to start shouting if he wanted to go. I would descend into a coughing fit the moment I tried, but that was beside the point.

DCI Harris did what I expected him to do and backed down. It made me despise him.

Thinking the discussion, if we could call it that, was over, Superintendent Charters said, "I hope you both feel better in the morning. You had a lucky escape. Sleep well."

Sleep well? I wanted to spit at his back as he left the room.

DCI Harris hung back, lingering in the doorway. "It's probably for the best if you drop the Daniel Mahony case, lads."

Patiently, Ashley pointed out, "He has no authority to demand that, sir."

"No, he's outside of my chain of command and our orders come from the Chief Constable for Kent, yet he has plenty of sway and can make our lives problematic if he wishes to do so."

He left a few moments later, offering his own get well wishes.

"The firefighters told me what you did." Ashley's statement came out of the blue. He'd waited until we were alone.

I was already facing him, so gave a shrug.

"I would get up and shake your hand, Tony. You deserve it, so I hope you'll take a raincheck."

"It was nothing. They carried you out of the building."

"Only because you fought them off to make sure they found me. That's how they described it."

I shrugged again and thought about getting out of bed. I felt fine. The cold had long since subsided and I was breathing normally. Sure, I felt like I needed to cough and thought I could hear a wheezy rattle coming from my chest, but it didn't seem like a big deal. Discharging myself would cause me some grief when my boss found out I had expressly disobeyed him, but with two weeks left did I really care?

"You hungry?" asked Ashley. "Tanya is stopping to pick up food on her way here. Can she get you something? It's the least I can do."

My stomach growled and the fight went out of me. The sensible thing was to stay in hospital until the doctors were content I could leave. Was I letting Elroy Stewart off the hook, though?

Not a chance.

Chapter 18

THE FOLLOWING MORNING, WHILE waiting for the doctors' rounds so we could be officially discharged, a face appeared outside the door. It was looking through to confirm it had the right place and upon seeing me it turned to speak to someone still out of sight.

Marvin Valmik, otherwise known as Marvin the Martian, let himself in with a breezy, "Good morning, chaps. Any lingering effects?"

Half a step behind him came a man I recognised but couldn't now name. I was in the process of shaking Marvin's hand when he came around him with his right arm extended.

"Chief Inspector Jim Riley," he said, jogging my memory.

Ashley lined up beside me, ignoring Marvin to shake the senior man's hand.

"You've been given the arson to investigate," I stated, adding two and two together. The fire was a deliberate attempt to murder two police officers. I was a little put out that the investigation had been given to a chief inspector and not a superintendent. It felt like they were downplaying the importance of our close brush with death. Like we weren't important enough to warrant a proper SIO.

Riley nodded. "That's right. I have your initial statements from last night, but now I need to grill you for more. Are you feeling up to it?"

I checked behind me and stepped back about a foot to lean against the edge of my bed. "Sure." I glanced at Ashley.

"Of course," he said, choosing to remain standing. "Is there any update on the whereabouts of Emily Harris?"

"Not yet," said Riley.

Marvin was too senior to be given second fiddle in this case, but like me was nearing retirement and had probably copped the task because he had nothing better to do. He had moved back a yard, giving the chief inspector the lead and remained quiet to watch and listen.

"The ports and airports have been alerted, so it's just a matter of time until she is picked up." He took out a notebook. "You reported last night that she called you. I need the approximate time."

"It was 1711hrs," I stated with confidence. "I was just about to knock off for the day when she called."

He nodded and made a note. "It was just you who spoke with her?"

"Yes. She called on a landline number and sounded nervous or scared." I remembered how I thought it was going to be our big breakthrough and that her statement would open the door for us to go after Elroy again. Now I believed the attack came about because Elroy or his people saw us at Rachael Weaver's house. Maybe they didn't know she was dead but should have been able to work it out from the coroner's van parked outside her property.

Elroy saw us there and devised a plan to take us out of the equation. I had nothing to back up my theory so kept it to myself though I suspected Ashley would be thinking the same thing.

"Well, the call came from within Ellison's Electricals, but she doesn't work there in any official capacity and none of the staff have ever heard of her."

"There was evidence of a cleaner going through the place when we arrived. The vacuum cleaner was out, that sort of thing. Is it possible she was doing cash-in-hand work and the boss doesn't want to admit he was fiddling the tax man?"

Chief Inspector Riley looked up from his notes. "No, sorry. I had that thought myself, but the staff we interviewed all had the same story; that they do the cleaning on rotation as part of the job. If Emily Harris worked there, one of them would have recognised her photograph."

The update suggested an additional level of sophistication I hadn't given Elroy the credit for. He'd selected a location on short notice, broke in, had Emily make the call, whether under duress or willingly, assembled a team, for they hit the front and back exits at the same time, plus someone had to find the stacks of newspapers ... Chances are he was familiar with the location and its closing time in advance but he still had to put it all together in just a few hours.

Riley had more questions for us, but our answers didn't help him. I got a call from Emily, and we walked into a trap. We didn't see anyone or hear anyone and were very lucky to be alive.

There were three officers working under the chief inspector, including Marvin. They didn't have a whole lot to go on and had to tread lightly around their central suspect, Elroy Stewart.

I never questioned whether he was behind it. He had to be. Just as he was behind the car that hit Ashley even if he wasn't the one behind the wheel.

Riley and his team would investigate the whereabout of Elroy and his known associates at the time of the arson, but I doubted they would have much luck. If we knew anything about him, it was Elroy's proclivity for lining up his alibis first.

Chapter 19

Shortly after Marvin and the chief inspector departed, we were discharged with instructions to report to our GPs if we were at all concerned. We were also to take it easy, but that didn't mean we couldn't go into work if we wanted to.

"I'm going home," Ashley told me, heading for Tanya's car. She had returned this morning to collect him. There was a squad car waiting for us and they would have delivered him to his door, but he was happier to travel with his fiancée. "I'll clean myself up and head back to the nick this afternoon. You'll take a couple of days, right?"

He fully expected me to take as much time off as I could get. A month ago I would have, but if I wasn't in work, he would have freedom to delve into the Bruce Denton case without my oversight.

I had to word my response carefully.

"No, I'm not going to take any time off. But look, do an old man a favour. Let's both just have a day, eh?" I had chosen to wait until he had the door to Tanya's car open. I met her for the first time last night and could see why he was marrying her. She was drop dead gorgeous with an amazing figure and a killer smile. She is also the rule maker in their house. There would be kids at some point, and I hoped for his sake they were boys. In an all-girl house he would be screwed.

I crouched a little so I could see in and say hello.

Tanya waved back at me with a cheery, "Good morning," which she followed by asking Ashley, "Did I just hear him ask to take a day? You're not thinking of going in today, are you?"

"Crime never sleeps, babe," Ashley delivered the line, clearly one he'd used before, in a gruff Batman voice. He knew he was going to lose, but wanted to make a point. Switching to a normal tone, he added, "We are getting close on two cases, angel. Driving the investigation forward now could make all the difference."

My lips twitched with the desire to point out that we were precisely nowhere with both our current cases. Emily Harris hadn't returned home and there was no CCTV footage to show who set the electrical wholesalers ablaze with us in it. With Rachael Weaver dead and Christine Westbury unwilling to talk, the only lead we had was the photograph. I could see where that led me later, but there was no reason to get excited just because no one thought to check who was behind the camera twenty years ago.

I closed my mouth without saying anything. Not because I was prepared to back down on taking the rest of the day off, but because I knew Tanya would say it so much better.

"I took the day off to be with you, Ashley. You were almost torched last night and spent the night having oxygen therapy. You are not going to work today." It was a statement. The kind that wives make where you stand more chance of winning a headbutt contest against a charging rhino than you do of changing their minds.

Ashley chose to demonstrate his lack of understanding by opening his mouth. I mean, he didn't get to speak but the intent was clearly there.

Tanya saw his lips move and said, "No." It was the kind of 'No' that is the verbal equivalent of cutting off a body part using an axe. Once the axe has swung, there is no unswinging it.

Looking a little lost and a touch embarrassed, as though this isn't the way it is for all men (except the sociopathic ones who think women should be subservient), Ashley turned to face me.

"Sure, Tony, let's take a day. That sounds good." He didn't mean it but had enough common sense to accept it was happening. "I'll see you tomorrow morning then?"

I held out my hand to shake. "We came close to buying it last night, kid." I hadn't called him kid since the first day we met. He called me out on it and our partnership has grown since, but it felt natural now and he let it pass without comment. "Enjoy a day with your lady. Tomorrow we can dig into Elroy Stewart again. Quietly, of course, but we'll get him."

Ashley gripped my hand hard, his eyes boring into mine. We were on the same page and if I could keep him on my side maybe he would be more inclined to listen when I said it was time to close the Bruce Denton case for good. Who knows, maybe almost dying would turn out to be a good thing.

I watched Tanya drive across the carpark before slipping into the passenger seat of the waiting squad car. My trusty old Vauxhall had already been delivered to my house, the nick rallying to help one of their own because that's what we do.

Sitting quietly in the car as we made our way back through the light morning traffic from Canterbury to the coast, I lined up my plan for the day. Ashley wouldn't go to work and with Tanya hovering over him, I doubted he would be able to work from home either.

However, Mary wouldn't impose the same restrictions on me. Not with the threat of permanent incarceration hanging over my head.

Chapter 20

MARY MADE ME A slap-up breakfast brunch thing when I got home. I told her not to come to the hospital the previous evening once we were settled onto the ward, not that I could have stopped her if she had been determined, but it seemed pointless. I was to be released in the morning and didn't want her driving on winding country roads in the dark.

Belly full to bursting, I then soaked in the bath for forty minutes, reading a book on my tablet. I couldn't recall the last time I had taken a bath during the day. It was nearly noon by the time I got back downstairs, dressed and ready to do something productive.

I could have slumped into an armchair and spent the afternoon watching reruns of Midsomer Murders, but I couldn't get Daniel Mahony and Elroy Stewart out of my head. In all my years as a cop and a detective, I have never really felt threatened. There were one or two incidents over the years where a suspect chose to fight rather than fold, but it never felt like I was about to come to serious harm, let alone die. Yet, since we started looking into who killed Daniel Mahony, my partner had been run down, we had a non-molestation order against us that prevented either one of us from going within a hundred feet of Elroy Stewart, and we almost burned to death last night when a person we could connect with Elroy lured us into a trap.

Ashley was going to drop it; I had seen that in his eyes and heard it in his tone. He had his career ahead of him, but I didn't. I found it most liberating. Not that I was about to confront Elroy. That would just get me arrested – ironic, isn't it? No, I was going to find the chink in his armour. There had to be one.

At my desk in the back bedroom, I took out the photograph – the one that kept him out of jail the first time. Boots the Chemist is a thriving business with a store in every town. I wasn't convinced they still offered the ability to print photographs; my experience is that no one really does that anymore. I was wrong though. Searching online I not only found that it was still a thing but that the local branch in Herne Bay had a pair of machines that could dispense my pictures if I so chose.

"Mary?" I called through the house. She was downstairs somewhere. I called again with just as much success and went to look for her. At the bottom of the stairs I called her name again and when I still got no response I racked my brains trying to recall if she said she had to go out for something.

The sound of the back door opening pulled my head and eyes in that direction just in time to see her arrive in from the garden.

"Where did you go?" I asked, taking in her slipper-clad feet and lack of coat.

She held up a bunch of odd looking green leafy things. "I'm making a sausage casserole. I needed herbs."

The garden has and always will be Mary's domain. I will mow the lawn when instructed to do so, and have silently suffered my way around plenty of garden centres, but planting things that will grow and then die has never interested me. Also, when I have tried to help because Mary wanted to grow peas or broad beans – two of my favourites – the crops always fail.

"I need to go into town," I announced.

"Oh, good. I'll get my coat."

I had a prepared speech to argue with her about why I needed to go and how I felt absolutely fine. Her instant agreement threw me completely.

"I'm sorry, what?"

Mary kicked off her slippers and put the herbs on her butcher's block. "I need to go to the bank for a start. I've been putting that off for days and then I want to pop into M&S to look for some mushrooms. And you can take me for a slice of cake somewhere since we'll be in town together for the first time in months."

"It hasn't been that long, love," I protested but my words fell on deaf ears. Mary was on her way to the front door to fetch her coat. We were going into town together whether I liked it or not, but since that suited my needs, I wasn't about to protest.

Chapter 21

ASHLEY PUT UP WITH being mothered until a little after lunch, not that he would dare to voice his thoughts within Tanya's earshot. She had work to do, even if the firm she worked for had given her the day off, so he waited until she drifted into the home office, then picked up his phone and laptop.

Like Tony, he wanted to get Elroy Stewart, but he was prepared to be patient about it. Tony didn't have the time to be patient, whereas Ashley knew he could circle back to the local kingpin in six months or a year. If he let emotion rule his head, he would find himself disobeying direct orders and that wasn't how a person found themselves in line for their next promotion. He had a lot of rungs to climb and was far too focused on where he was going to let one criminal with murderous intentions ruin it all.

So he ignored the Daniel Mahony enquiry, just as he was told to, and turned his attention to the old favourite instead. The video of the woman walking arm in arm with Bruce Denton appeared to be worthless. The line set up to receive calls got a whole glut of them in the first few days after the video was shown. As expected, they were all dead ends and the frequency of people phoning in had dwindled to nothing.

It was a surprise because Tony had seemed so certain she would be recognised. In fact, he'd acted as though the case was all but closed. Why was that? He had grown to ... well, not like his partner. He and Tony were not about to start hanging out after work, but he could appreciate him. Yet the worry that Tony was hiding something persisted.

From Vicky he knew about Bryan Hayworth, the other detective sergeant at the nick in Herne Bay. He was yet to make contact, but perhaps now was the right time. He had already tracked down the man's details. Knowing his voice would carry through the house, even if he closed the living room door, Ashley figured it was better to just make the call and deal with Tanya afterward if she chose to be upset that he was working after saying he wouldn't.

Now retired, Bryan Hayworth was sixty-eight years old and living in Rochester, some thirty miles to the north. Ashley dialled his number and waited for it to connect.

"Bryan Hayworth." The voice, a strong, deep baritone, filled his ear. It had an almost musical edge to it, making Ashley wonder if the man was a good singer.

"Good afternoon, this is Detective Sergeant Ashley Long." He paused for a second to let that sink in. "I'm assigned to a task-force investigating old cases and I hoped I might be able to pick your brain about a murder that occurred in Herne Bay thirty years ago."

"Thirty years ago?" Bryan repeated the words not as a question, but with a wistful air as though delving back through his memories. "You mean Bruce Denton, don't you."

"Indeed, sir. The case has been reopened after some new evidence came to light. Have you by any chance seen the video clip that's being shown on the news?"

"Oh, I never watch the news. It's far too depressing. What's the clip?"

Ashley confirmed Bryan had an internet connection and got him to access the clip online. He had to wait while the older man navigated his way to it and again while he tried to get it to work. Then, in the background and to himself, Ashley got to hear the retired cop mutter in wonder at the old piece of footage.

"So this is what Tony lost. You say someone found it in a bog? How the heck did it get there?"

How indeed.

"Do you recognise the woman with Bruce Denton?" Ashley held his breath.

Bryan made him wait, playing the clip two more times before concluding, "No, sorry."

Ashley hadn't expected anything different, and had other questions lined up to ask. He was just checking his notes when Bryan started to talk again.

"But there is something very familiar about her."

"Familiar?"

"Yeah. Don't ask me how but I think I know her. There're no angles that show her face, right?"

"I'm afraid not." The case might be closed if they could see her face.

At the other end of the line, Bryan huffed and grumbled, the verbal equivalent of scratching one's head.

"I'm sure you've spoken with Tony Heaton about this. What did he say?"

"Actually, we are partners. He's investigating with me."

"You're kidding. He's not retired yet? And they haven't kicked him out? That's incredible."

"How so?" Vicky said DS Hayworth caused division at the nick when he suggested the killer could be a cop. Ashley understood why he made that conclusion and also why every other cop would have argued against it.

"Look, if you're investigating the murder of Bruce Denton, then I'm sure you have the case file and have read it cover to cover. You sound like a bright kid. I made myself very unpopular by pointing out how the murder scene was so clean we had to consider that someone from law enforcement could be behind it."

"I read that."

"Yeah, well did you read that Tony turned everyone against me and had me hounded out of my own nick? I ended up taking a job with the Met in London where I wasn't known. Tony made it impossible for me to stay in Herne Bay even though I was technically his superior."

"How did he do that? What tactics did he employ?" This was the first he'd heard of it, but he could check with Vicky later.

Was Bryan being accurate with his accusations, or exaggerating them?

"Oh, it was all verbal," Bryan sighed. "Tony twisted the things I said. If I walked into a room, he would tell everyone to watch their backs. There were a few incidents where notes found their way into people's bags. The note would say something like 'I'm watching you'. I never sent them, but he made everyone believe I was behind it. I think he was the culprit."

"Did the two of you have a bad relationship beforehand?"

"No. Not really. He was the junior detective. I remember when he was promoted to DS. The moment I heard about it I went to shake his hand. It was obvious to anyone he was going places. Hey, if he's working with you on this case now, what rank is he? Is he the senior investigating officer?"

"No, Tony is still a sergeant." It surprised Ashley that Bryan didn't know.

"Well, I'll be. I had him pegged to get to superintendent at least."

The subject was interesting, but they were massively off topic. To wrap it up, Ashley said, "He wouldn't let the Bruce Denton case go and from what I understand it ruined his career. But I want to go back to your thoughts on who the killer could have been. If you thought it was someone in law enforcement, was there anyone connected to the victim?" Ashley had already asked a similar question of Tony who assured him there was no one who fit the bill, but he wanted to hear it from someone different.

Bryan didn't answer straight away, but after a few seconds, he said, "No. Not really."

"Not really?" He was going to have to do a lot better than that.

"Look, I'm not happy about discussing this over the phone. Can you meet me?"

Ashley grimaced, his frustration rising. He felt fine. Certainly well enough to drive to Rochester but didn't feel like having that argument with Tanya.

"I can't come to you. I'm at home convalescing after suffering smoke inhalation last night. Can you come to me?"

Ashley expected kick back, but the old cop said he had nothing better to do. He would leave in the next ten minutes and be with him in under an hour. When they ended the call, Ashley went to let Tanya know they would have a guest.

She narrowed her eyes at him. "I figured that was a work call I could hear. Which case is it for?"

Ashley told her about all his cases, but only in broad brush terms – the sort of information that was available on the internet.

"That old murder in Herne Bay. The one my partner was involved in."

"Oh, yes. The one with the video. You haven't said anything about that in days. Did you find the woman?"

"No. Well, not yet, I suppose I should say." He didn't want to sound defeatist.

A slight frown creased her perfect features. "You were so confident before."

"I was," Ashley replied automatically, but was that right? It wasn't his confidence so much as Tony's.

"Would you like a cup of tea?" she asked, getting out of her chair.

"Um, yes, please," he said, deep in thought and distracted.

Tanya collected some pages from her printer and made sure they were straight and even before picking up her stapler. It misfired and she cursed, flicking the top open with a delicate finger to reveal there were no staples inside.

Voicing his thoughts, Ashley said, "Tony was convinced it would blow the case wide open. It ..." he stopped talking mid-sentence. Thinking back to the first time they watched the footage at the nick after the tech boys had done their best with it, Tony had been as white as a sheet. That was nothing unusual when it came to the Bruce Denton case, but looking back at it now, it was as though he'd been terrified the woman would be identified.

Tanya bent over to root around in a cupboard. She did it on purpose, acting sexy to show off the shape of her long legs and derriere instead of simply crouching to fetch the staples. She shot him a wink when she caught him looking.

Repeating his previous sentence, he said, "Tony thought it would blow the case wide open, but you've seen the footage. It shows a woman who Tony said would be recognised, but no one has any idea why he thought that because we never see her face."

Tanya wasn't sure what she could say to help, but thinking aloud said, "Sounds like he could tell who she was from behind."

Chapter 22

MARY INSISTED I ACCOMPANY her to the bank and was very pleased to bump into Jane Hartley, a woman she went to school with, so she could show off how close we still were as a couple. I was dragged around M&S where we somehow spent more than fifty pounds despite only going in for mushrooms, but when Mary remembered it was my idea to go into town, she decided she had more interesting things to do than come to Boots.

That was fine by me.

Walking into the shop, I spotted the photobooth things immediately. I guess I had seen them every time I walked in for the last however many years, but never really noticed what they were. There were two machines of which one was unoccupied. A likely looking sales assistant was helping a middle-aged man at the one machine in use. He looked about as bewildered as I would be.

Naturally, the assistant was about twelve, okay eighteen, but hoping he would be able to help me anyway, I went to stand at the machine next to the one in use, effectively trapping the poor boy between me and his current customer. I gave him a minute and when he turned to see if I needed any assistance, I showed my warrant card.

All colour drained from his face and I thought he was going to faint. Certain from his reaction he had something worth hiding, I nevertheless said, "I just have a few questions about some photographs that were printed using one of these machines."

"Oh," said the boy, still looking terrified and not very relieved at all.

"Yes," I produced the photograph of Elroy and friends, turning it to show the faint line of text running across the back. It was inside a clear plastic bag to protect it, but he could see the words clearly enough. "Is there any way to trace where this was printed and when?"

The boy squinted at the letters and numbers. "How old is this?" he asked in the tone of a person who couldn't yet conceive of time in the form of decades. To his mind it was so old the technology used to make it probably involved two men and a cranking handle.

I turned the photograph over to show him the date on the front. He actually sniggered but was able to wipe the amusement from his face when he looked up at me.

"I'll need to ask my supervisor. I'm not sure records will go back this far."

He scurried away too fast for the customer still trying to print his pictures. Seeing the young man go, he lifted his arm, his fingers clutching the air, but he made no attempt to call him back.

Catching my eye, he said, "I swear they keep inventing new things just so anyone over the age of fifteen won't be able to keep up." I thought perhaps I was going to have to engage in polite conversation, but he turned back to his machine and continued to poke the buttons, tutting and sighing when it persisted in failing to do what he expected.

I wandered a few feet away, diminishing the chance that he might ask for my help. My expectation was that I would be kept waiting, or that the kid's terror at seeing my identification would convince him to disappear behind the scenes and never return. He proved me wrong in less than a minute, reappearing from whence he went with a woman in tow.

Where he was skinny to the point of emaciation, she had a full figure with wide hips. She was taller, broader, and wearing the

Boots version of a suit with nylons on her legs plus a pair of newish low-heeled shoes.

The young man got her close enough and peeled away to do something else when he saw me coming.

"Hello," I said, flashing my warrant card again. "Detective Sergeant Heaton. I have a couple of questions about a photograph." I showed it to her.

The first thing she did was snigger, but she quickly apologised. "Sorry, Nathan told me it was a really old picture. He made it sound like it was pre-war or something, but that's millennials for you. What is it you want to know?"

I flipped it over to show her the numbers and letters on the back. "Anything you can tell me would be helpful. Specifically, I would like to know who paid for it to be printed. Is that information likely to be available?" While the person who paid wasn't necessarily the same person who took the picture, I hoped it would be close enough to not matter.

Would the name help me? That I did not know, but at this precise moment, until they found Emily Harris and I could squeeze her for information, I didn't have a whole lot of other leads to pursue.

According to the badge pinned to her lapel, the woman's name was Leigh Sage and she was the store's deputy manager. I figured, given her age, which was somewhere in her late forties, and her seniority, I was unlikely to find anyone better suited to provide answers I could trust.

"Well, since everything went digital in the nineties, in theory at least, every scrap of information is recorded somewhere. However, people still paid with cash in 2003. Certainly a lot more regularly than they do now, so unless they used a card there will be no record."

I should have expected that to be the case.

"However ..." Leigh had a thoughtful look on her face. She turned to walk back through the store, leaving me behind until she paused to make sure I was following. "I'm not promising anything, but I think the letters and numbers on the back will tell us what machine was used and where. Actually, I'm sure that's the case, but I can't say what good this will do us. Can I ask what this is about?"

"Sorry, it's for an ongoing case. I can't talk about it."

"Oh," she eyed me sceptically, probably wondering how it could be an ongoing case if the photo was more than two decades old. Taking my answer at face value, she led me through a door marked 'staff only'. It led to a corridor and then to an office.

The office had no window and was a plain square with a desk facing a wall with a computer and screen. It was a depressing space, but clearly one Leigh spent time in because there was a picture of her with some kids next to the keyboard.

"Please, have a seat." She indicated a tired chair in the opposite corner. "This shouldn't take too long."

She hid the keyboard and screen from me while she typed in a password but settled into her chair after that. Tapping at a few keys and moving the mouse brought up screens of numbers, none of which I could decipher, but two minutes of silent patience were rewarded when she announced, "Yes, this was printed at the store in Whitstable."

"Super." I dared to hope I might be onto something. "What else can you tell me?"

"Huh? Oh, about the person who printed them?"

"Yes, please."

Leigh spun her chair through a quarter circle, so she wasn't quite facing me, but wasn't facing the desk either.

"Sorry," she made an apologetic face. "That sort of information isn't shown." Seeing my disappointment, she said, "But I can see what else we can discover. Like I said earlier, if they paid with a card, we should still have their details on record."

"But not here?" I guessed.

"No, sorry. I can contact head office, but it will take a couple of days for them to run the request. Then there's the small question of GDPR."

The general data protection regulation, which came into effect in 2018 immediately made police work harder because it created a wall of protection behind which criminals could hide. I could get around it but would probably need a court order to have the information released. To my mind such rules shouldn't apply to the police, but they do.

I could see I wasn't going to get any further today, but said, "Leigh, anything you can find out about the person who printed the pictures will help." I still doubted the name would lead me anywhere, but it felt good to be doing something.

After thanking Leigh for her help and confirming she had my contact information, I left the store and headed back to my car. On the way a nagging sensation arose. I was forgetting something, but try as I might I couldn't figure out what. I sifted through my thoughts on both the Bruce Denton and Daniel Mahony cases without producing a single idea about what might have slipped my mind. Thinking maybe it was Emily Harris troubling me, I dialled Doris at the station. I'm supposed to call the dispatch desk for updates, but Doris always knows more than anyone else.

Doris confirmed there was no change in the status of Emily Harris. She had gone to ground. I hoped that wasn't literally where she would be found.

"Tony!" called a familiar voice. I had just ended my call and was almost at the carpark. The sound of my name being called made me freeze, and I exaggerated the motion so it looked like someone had just hit me with a futuristic freeze ray. I had one foot off the ground, mid-stride.

The thing I had forgotten was my wife.

"Had you forgotten me?" she demanded, knowing full well that I had. If she hadn't called my name I would have driven home and only remembered her when there was no one to make dinner. I'm not a chauvinist or misogynist, honest. I'm just not very good in the kitchen and I'm distracted.

"No, my love. How could I ever?"

Mary narrowed her eyes, not believing me for one second.

"Take me home, Tony Heaton. You need to go back to resting."

Chapter 23

Tanya got to the door first when Ashley's plan to greet Bryan as he arrived was defeated by his need to visit the smallest room. Cursing as he urged his bladder to void itself faster, Ashley arrived back on the ground floor of their house to find his fiancée leading the retired cop through the house.

"And he wanted to see you today?" Tanya was asking.

"This shouldn't take long, my love," Ashley cut in quickly.

Picking up on the obvious tension in the air, Bryan looked from one to the other. "Um, I can return another time if now isn't convenient."

"Oh, there's no need to leave," said Tanya, giving Ashley eyes that could cut through steel. "Ashley knows what's best for him. No need to listen to the silly doctors."

"Oh. Yes, you did say you were at home to convalesce."

Ashley had no desire to upset or antagonise his lady, but it was done now, and it wasn't as though he was going to exacerbate his condition just by talking.

"It's fine," he insisted. "Seriously. I'm fine. Staying at home is merely a precaution. I will be back at work tomorrow."

Tanya shot him another look, but he could tell she didn't really mean it. She was teasing him more than she was serious.

"Come through to the lounge," he beckoned Bryan to follow. "Can I offer you a coffee or something else?"

"Just water, please." He didn't want to find himself nursing a hot drink when their conversation ended. He didn't expect to be at the young detective's house for long.

"I'll get it," said Tanya, who was in the kitchen making herself a drink.

Taking a spot opposite Ashley on the three-seater leather sofa, Bryan started talking before he'd fully settled.

"You wanted to know more about my thoughts on Bruce Denton. Tell me how well you know Shakespeare."

Ashley blinked, certain he must have misheard.

"Me thinks she doth protest too much," quoted Bryan.

Or rather, misquoted, Ashley silently acknowledged. He knew the quote well enough from his English Literature studies. He'd received an A Star grade at A-Level and Hamlet featured prominently in his final year. They had even performed the play, though it was over a series of weeks in the classroom and they were largely hamming it up.

"Ok," he said, waiting for the retired detective to make his point.

"Look, I'm not going to point the finger, but when I first suggested it could be a cop or at least someone who knew law enforcement, crime scene forensics and such, there were a lot of dissenting voices. I already told you I was pretty much hounded out of the nick and had to transfer to London, but the loudest voice was always Tony's. So put that together."

Far from not pointing the finger, Bryan Hayworth had done precisely that.

"You think Tony could be Bruce Denton's killer?"

Bryan, who was sitting forward in his chair, lifted his arms in a 'beats me' gesture. "Look, I don't know. But you've read how clean the crime scene was. No physical evidence whatsoever. That's no accident." Bryan stabbed the air with an index finger as he made his point. "Now add to that uncomfortable fact that the one person pushing back hardest against what was an obvious conclusion was the man running the investigation. Oh, I know he was just a sergeant and the person actually running it was the nick's superintendent, but that's not how it worked back then. Superintendent Smart didn't like to get his hands dirty. He controlled things from afar. So it was Tony running it right from the start. And let's not forget that the one piece of evidence that might have opened the case up was lost. By Tony," he concluded as though nailing the lid shut on the case.

Ashley's mind raced. He'd given credence to the idea that the killer could be a cop. Like Bryan said, it was an obvious conclusion to draw from the crime scene. Yet, Tony had been trying to catch the killer for most of the last thirty years, so clearly he wasn't guilty. All the same, there were discrepancies in the casefile, he missed out what might yet prove to be a vital clue when he failed to record information Vicky reported, and he was certain the woman in the video would be recognised even though her face was never in shot.

"Yes, he did, but we have the camcorder and footage now. You said earlier that you thought she looked familiar. I'm going to play the video again." He flicked on the TV and selected YouTube from the list of Apps.

He needed a few seconds to bring up the right clip, and it started playing just as Tanya walked in. She had a glass of water in her hand.

All three watched the short clip in silence.

"That's the mystery woman?" Tanya asked, selecting a coaster from a drawer and placing the water on the side table next to their guest.

Ashley looked at Bryan. "Could she be a cop? Or someone working in forensics?"

Bryan slumped back a little into the sofa. "I don't know," he admitted. "It could be. There were plenty of female cops in the nineties. A lot more than there were a decade before when I first joined the force, that's for sure. I don't recognise her though. Not from a few seconds of footage. Is there any more?"

Ashley shook his head. "Nope. That's all we have."

They chatted for a little while longer, Bryan reaffirming his belief that a cop was behind the brutal bludgeoning more than once. But he had nothing to back up his claim that wasn't already in the case notes.

It was after four when Ashley waved his guest goodbye, closed the door, and leaned against it, his brain ablaze with thoughts that made his stomach swirly. It was the thing Tanya said that bothered him most because it made complete sense. He spent enough time looking at his fiancée's derriere to be able to recognise it from behind.

Troubled by a thought he didn't want to be true, he went back to his laptop and opened the list of VRNs Tony sent him. He had planned to interrogate it when he got home last night, but the brush with death meant that never happened and almost two days had gone by since he received it.

The light sound of Tanya's footsteps coming his way made him look up before she appeared.

"Any thoughts on dinner?" she asked.

They tended to split cooking duties. Her job as a lawyer, and still a junior at the firm, meant she worked longer hours than either of them liked, but that fitted well with his chosen profession. They made it work, but their evening meals were often something that was quick to throw together and eating at separate times was normal.

Today they could make a meal together, but Ashley sensed the question was loaded.

"I'm easy, babe. Shall we order food in? Or we could go out?" They tried to have a meal out at least once a week, but his schedule in recent weeks, and his time in hospital after the car hit him, meant their last trip to a restaurant was almost three weeks ago.

"Out sounds good. If you are up to it?" she added a quick caveat. He still wore a cast on one arm, limped a little from the bruising to his hip and pelvis, and had just been released from hospital after suffering smoke inhalation. She wanted to visit the little Thai place in the next town but wasn't about to push Ashley to get dressed up if he didn't feel ready.

"Sounds good," he said, bringing a smile to Tanya's face, which was his constant aim. "Six-ish?"

"I was thinking later."

They settled on seven for dinner, which sounded like an adult time to be out if still a little early. When Tanya returned to her work, Ashley began to scrutinise the file of vehicle registrations. It was a task of elimination, some of which Tony had already done for him, so the list now only contained men from thirty years ago who were registered keepers of vehicles in the area with a VRN that ended with FUN.

The email from Tony said he had eliminated everyone over sixty. The description given to Vicky Hopper was that of a man in his twenties or thirties. Leaving in those in their forties and fifties was probably unnecessary, but eyewitness reports can be shockingly unreliable, so he knew why his partner included them.

Bored with the task before he even started, Ashley logged into the central database and typed in the first name on the list.

When it returned no record to show the man had no criminal past – just as he expected ninety-nine percent of the names would – he moved to a new database. There were plenty of ways to find information on a person, so cross-referencing what he found against what he knew about Bruce – where he worked and lived, where he went to school, et cetera, he annotated the name as 'unlikely' and moved on.

It was boring, routine police work, the sort of thing an underling ought to be tasked with. However, the downside of being assigned to the cold case taskforce was he had no one to whom he could delegate. So he was stuck with it. All he needed was for one name to show a plausible link to the victim, and he would have an avenue to explore.

Unless ...

Ashley stopped typing. Unless the connection wasn't to the victim but to the woman in the video. If that was the case, the list he had was mostly useless because he had no clue who the woman was. It was all so frustrating.

The original investigation fell apart when Tony lost the camcorder. That was how he explained it, but it looked more like they never had a case to begin with. There was no real suspect who managed to slip through the net due to lack of evidence. There was no evidence.

But the woman ...

Pushing back from the keyboard, he knew there was another person he was yet to talk to about the victim or the woman in the video. Bruce had a fiancée until four months before he was murdered. From the notes in the casefile Ashley knew she was interviewed at the time for completeness only and was never suspected of any involvement in her former lover's death, but it didn't say why they split up.

They didn't have the video to show her thirty years ago, but if their relationship ended because he was seeing another woman, would she know her name?

There was no number listed for Angela Wilcox and Ashley thought it doubtful it was still her last name, but it wouldn't take too long to track her down. Simple arithmetic made her close to sixty now, assuming she was roughly Bruce's age or a little younger. Tony probably knew if she had married, what her name was now, and chances were that he had contact information for her. But he didn't want to ask Tony.

After the conversation with Tony's former colleague, Bryan Hayworth, and the sense that Tony knew the identity of the woman in the video, he was going to play his cards close to his chest from now on.

Chapter 24

I SLEPT BETTER THAN I had in weeks and awoke to find my alarm clock was one minute from going off. I clicked the switch to the left, silencing it before it could launch its morning offensive. Mary was a lump in the duvet, a mess of blonde hair hiding her face. I could hear her breathing gently in and out as she continued to sleep.

I slipped out of bed, gathering clothes and dressing in the bathroom once I was clean and shaved. I expected my movements would wake her, but she didn't appear to have twitched when I poked my head back around the corner of the bedroom door to check on her.

Downstairs I made tea and chose scrambled eggs on buttered white toast for breakfast. I wouldn't leave without waking Mary to say goodbye, but she hadn't slept any better than me in recent weeks, so I made as little noise as possible, quietly watching the local news on my laptop while I ate.

The biggest story was the fire at Ellison's Electricals in Whitstable. The report stated there were no victims, which meant the reporters arrived too late and the firefighters had been briefed not to mention the two police officers who were almost extra crispy. Listed as a probable arson, the report simply said the police were investigating. They had a photograph of the burnt-out unit, another of the firefighters fighting the fire which someone local must have taken on their mobile, and finally one showing Marvin and Jim Riley.

When the clock read quarter to eight, I made another cup of tea and delivered it to Mary, who murmured her thanks in a sleepy voice. I kissed the top of her head where it poked above the duvet. She had it tucked tight around her as though the house was cold. My retirement was nine days away. Nine working days, that is. Twelve actual days, but my official retirement, by which I mean the last day they paid me, would occur almost two months later. Accrued annual leave, sick days, and what people call gardening leave so those deemed too old to serve, were allowed time to find a new job, meant I was just twelve days from walking out of Herne Bay nick for the last time.

Was that enough to see the end of the Bruce Denton case? Could I convince Ashley to give it all up by then? Was I going to have to do something drastic to stop him?

The last question reverberated inside my skull, reminding me that I could have left him to die in the fire. Left him? I could have pushed him. I could have ended his life two nights ago and woken yesterday morning certain in the knowledge that the case had died with him. No one else would ever pick it up, but I hadn't been able to make myself do it. Instinct kicked in and I saved him instead.

Whether I would come to regret that was yet to be decided.

I drove to work to find Ashley already there. He was at his desk, and so focused on his laptop he didn't look up until I was standing right over him. At that point he sighed and sat back in his chair. Using both hands, he scratched at his scalp like someone wishing they had long hair so they could pull it out.

"I'm nearly through that list of VRNs and none of the owners look likely. I can't find one who appears to have a connection to Bruce Denton, but it occurred to me yesterday that he might not be the one we should be checking against."

I guessed what he was not saying. "You mean the woman?"

Ashley dropped his hands so they were resting on the arms of his chair and swivelled it around so he faced me. To avoid his eyes – I knew he wanted to see what they did when I spoke – I turned to my own desk and opened my bag.

"Tony, why did you think everyone would know who she was?"

I lifted my eyebrows, my face side on to his so he would see it but not be able to judge what the rest of my features were doing.

"As I recall, I said that someone would recognise her. Not everyone."

"Even so, what made you think that? The video never shows her face, yet you were convinced we would have her name in no time at all."

I placed my bag on the floor and turned around to meet his gaze. I didn't want him to think I was avoiding his eyes and was prepared to lie without letting it show.

"It was the thing that killed the case, Ashley. My dominant memory from the first time I saw the footage was that we were going to have a big break in the case. You know well enough how this case has affected me. Seeing her again after so many years threw me for a twist. Thirty years ago I think she would have been identified in a heartbeat. That feeling stayed with me."

Ashley stared at me. He wasn't buying it. I could tell. There was something going on behind his eyes, a question he wanted to ask but couldn't. It sent a wave of concern to my belly.

Turning away or dropping my eyes would have sent the wrong signal, so I held his gaze, daring him to speak the words in his head. I don't think he suspected there was anything or anyone missing from the list of VRNs, but he was questioning who the people on it should be connected to. That was fine. It was still the wrong question.

To hammer home a point, I said, "I told you the list would get us nowhere. The witness statements were misleading thirty years ago, and nothing had changed. Were there men in their cars in the street? Almost certainly, yes. But they were in different cars, and they were different men. I draw the same conclusion now that I did back then: it's a total red herring. Now, shall we try something different or are you ready to accept there's no way to solve this case?"

Ashley's expression didn't change much, and he didn't answer my question. At least not straight away. His lips shifted, showing me that he was thinking. I wished I knew what he was thinking about, but I could guess. His questions about the woman, the way he worded them. He suspected ... something.

Then realisation hit me like a hammer blow to the chest, and I had to fake a coughing fit to cover up the sudden jolt of panic that shot through me. The colour had drained from my face. I felt it go.

Ashley got to his feet as I bent over the desk next to his and tried to get my breath.

"Hey, are you okay?" his concern was genuine. "Have you been coughing much?" He thought this was the aftereffects of the smoke.

I gave him a thumbs up, pretending that was the best I could manage, and fished in my bag for my bottle of water.

Ashley took it from me and got the lid off.

I continued the act, covering my sense of terror long enough for my rational side to catch up. If he knew anything, I would be in cuffs. So he didn't, but something had shifted.

Using my hands as though they were necessary to keep me moving, I clawed my way around the desk and slumped into the chair. "That caught me by surprise," I croaked.

"Have you been coughing much?" he repeated the question. It was one of the things the doctors told us to look for and to report.

"No," I shook my head and kept my face pointing downwards as I ran through what I might have missed. Who had he spoken to since I was last with him? "No, that's the first one like that." Gavin Dobbs came over to check on me, but I waved him away. "I'm fine." I looked up and around the room. Most of its occupants were looking my way. "Nothing to worry about. Just a guy who shouldn't have smoked in the eighties," I joked, hoping it would diffuse their interest.

It worked, but that left me with Ashley still watching my every move.

"So, going back to my question about Bruce Denton. What do you want to do? Do you want to keep going? There are other people we can talk to, but all we are really doing is wasting time when you could be solving one of the other cases."

I hadn't planned to take this strategy yet. I figured we were days away from Ashley accepting there were no threads at which he could tug, so I was supremely surprised when he nodded his head.

"Maybe, yeah. I still say no case is unsolvable ..."

"Tell that to the team who tried to catch Jack the Ripper."

"But," he carried on as though I hadn't spoken, "I'm starting to think you might be right. Maybe too much time has passed." He sought out my eyes, looking for me to respond.

Getting unsteadily to my feet, as though the coughing fit had been real and I was still recovering, I placed a hand on his shoulder.

"Sorry, Ashley. I wish it was different, but there never was any evidence. Unless a miracle happens and the woman comes forward, we have no leads to follow."

He nodded, accepting the truth for what it was.

Except I could tell he didn't.

Like me, he was lying.

It was subtle and he might have been able to hide it from me had he not been scrutinising me so intently when he asked about why I thought the woman would be recognised. He knew something. Or thought he did, which was just as dangerous. But could he know it was Mary? Merely thinking the question drove another shard of icy terror through my heart.

He broke through my thoughts when he said, "We should pick another case."

I was so lost in my own head I grunted, "Huh?" before my brain caught up. "Oh, yeah. I guess if you are dropping Bruce Denton," which I didn't for one moment believe he was, "and we are barred from the Daniel Mahony case, I guess we need something new. You're the one with the list. Don't tell me you haven't already got one in mind."

"Actually, I do, but it will take a day or more to get the evidence delivered from central storage. Plus, we need to send back what we have on both Bruce and Daniel Mahony."

"We also need to follow up with the coroner about Rachael Weaver," I reminded him. Was it really only two days ago that we were in her house? It felt like too much had happened since then. I remained doubtful her death was going to prove to be anything other than a poorly timed ironic coincidence for our investigation. Had it come at the hands of Elroy Stewart or one of his minions, they would have needed to know about the phone call where she conceded to tell the truth, but the forensics team had found no listening devices in her house.

It was possible the killer removed them after the deed to better cover their tracks, but I doubted it.

I watched Ashley close his laptop and pack his things away. We were heading to the coroner's office.

Chapter 25

ASHLEY FOLLOWED TONY FROM the nick, trying hard not to stare at the back of his head. Thirty-six hours ago his partner saved his life. There was no doubt in his mind that the only reason he was still breathing was Tony's decision to drag him out of the fire. How could he be thinking the things he was thinking? Tony had to be on the level. Yet more and more, Ashley worried that he wasn't. It made his head swim.

Tony knew who the woman was. Ever since Tanya said it, Ashley hadn't been able to shift the belief, but when he posed the question, not that he did so directly, Tony faked a coughing fit to cover his reaction. Ashley was sure of it.

Worse yet, he thought he knew who the woman was. The ages were about right. Not that he could put an accurate age to the woman in the video, but she was somewhere in her twenties or very early thirties and that was bang on for Tony's wife. She was about the right height and the hair colour matched too. But why would it be Mary Heaton?

The answer to that was simple enough. She'd been having an affair and Tony found out. He bludgeoned his wife's lover to death in his own home and covered it up by making sure he was the investigating officer. It sent a chill down Ashley's spine. Variations of what could be the truth had kept him awake for most of the night, but was he wrong? Or had he spent the last month sitting next to a killer?

Pulse racing, Ashley knew he had to step carefully. Tony couldn't know what he suspected. Not that Ashley thought he was in any danger. The unpredictable nature of man aside, even with his arm in a cast and a slight limp, Tony was no match. They were on their way to visit the coroner, a task that could have been completed with a phone or video call if Tony wasn't so set in his ways. He liked to conduct his meetings face to face where he could get the measure of a person and gauge their responses to judge how much of what they said was true.

It would give him time to think, time to strategize. Now that he suspected Bryan Hayworth could be right, Ashley needed to dig a little deeper. The VRN check got him nowhere, but he'd let Tony perform it. How hard would it have been for him to fudge the result? Ashley's first action had to be rechecking the results, but he couldn't do that with Tony around.

Briefly, Ashley toyed with the idea of faking his own coughing fit, or stomach cramps, or anything that would excuse him from going to the coroner's officer. Certain Tony would see through it, or that he wasn't a good enough actor to make it look convincing, he followed his partner out to the car. Above all else, he needed to act normal. He could investigate later.

Chapter 26

SINCE WE COMPLETED OUR first case and found some common ground, Ashley and I have fallen into a relaxed partnership where we can chat amiably about something or nothing much whenever we are in the car. Not so today. Today there was nothing to talk about, just suspicious side glances until I could take it no more and picked a subject I knew I could use to distract him.

"What's the shortlist for the next case?" I wanted to ask him what he was thinking but I was too terrified he might just say it.

He shrugged; a two-shoulder act of indifference. He didn't want to talk, but had he not done so I would have pushed him.

"There are a few options. Grace Snoke is one that I would like to investigate."

"I remember the case," I said, glad to have words to fill the deafening silence.

He twisted in his seat to show me his surprise. "Were you involved?"

"Nah. It's just one of those cases that sticks in the head. The husband reported her missing and went on the news to do the press conference things, begging for anyone with information to dial the number on the screen, but when they found her body, he was the one they arrested."

"They never charged him though."

"That's because he didn't do it. At least, that was the conclusion the guys involved in the case reached. He looked good for it. He had a mistress, plus his wife was sucking him dry and had gained eighty pounds. He had motive to want to be rid of her, but the evidence was entirely circumstantial and his alibi – that he was with his mistress when his wife vanished – held up when CCTV footage was found of him taking her out to dinner. He was fifty miles away on a supposed business trip and couldn't have done it."

"That's what I read, too. So it's interesting because they weren't able to identify a second suspect. It would be a good one to solve, but I'm not sure where we would start."

This was better. He was talking to me about cold cases. I needed to figure out what he knew about Mary. Or whether he knew anything about Mary. Time to think would be good, but as much as anything, I wanted to get hold of his laptop and phone and see who he'd been talking to or what notes he might have made. If Ashley was with me, he couldn't poke his nose into my business, but that would change soon enough. If not before, I would lose track of him when the day ended.

Yet again, while he talked, I fretted about the very real possibility that my only way to escape justice was to kill him. A wave of revulsion turned my stomach.

"Are you okay?" he asked, noticing the grimace on my face.

"I ate too much for breakfast," I lied. "It's not sitting well."

He had nothing to say to that, and the roar of silence returned, filling my ears with its persistence. I could see his mind working, and despite telling myself I was just being paranoid, I knew he was thinking about Bruce Denton and what I might be hiding.

A few minutes later we arrived at the coroner's office in Whitstable. Traffic had been kind for once. Inside we were made to wait, but not for long. I thought I would have to fill the time with banal conversation or push him to expound his theories on where Emily Harris might be, but the coroner appeared sooner than I expected.

We didn't need to see Rachael's body; we saw it yesterday after all. Our visit was to discuss his findings. The scene of crime guys had found nothing to indicate there was another person in the house – no sign of forced entry, no footprints, so I expected to hear the same conclusion, even though it would help our cause if that were not the case.

"Sorry," he apologised, "She had a heart attack. It seems likely she was trying to get downstairs to find her phone or raise the alarm when she lost consciousness. I can't prove those elements, that's just conjecture," he pointed out, "but the bruising to her body aligns with a fall down the stairs and there are no marks to suggest she was moved forcibly from her bed and pushed. I believe she was set to be a key witness? Is that right?"

I nodded, and Ashley said, "We hoped she would be able to provide testimony that would lead to an important arrest."

His tone was filled with disappointment, and I knew he was kicking himself for allowing her to defer her statement until the morning after he spoke with her. Had he gone straight there and pushed, even if it was to be against Cindy's wishes, we would have her statement and that would change the whole case against Elroy Stewart.

When I heard she was dead, I assumed it was murder, another case of Elroy protecting his secret. If it was then he did a great job of covering his tracks because both the forensics team and the coroner were ruling death by misadventure.

Irked, but far too distracted by Ashley's behaviour and the sense of terror it gave me to put much thought to anything else, I suggested we return to the station. More than anything, I wanted to aim Ashley in the direction of a new case. He said he was ready to let Bruce Denton go, and though I didn't believe him, I had to act as if I did. I was calmer now, over the initial shock of realisation. It meant I could think more rationally. Back at the nick I would try to find a chance to check out his laptop and phone (if I could get around his passwords and facial recognition). Something had made him look my way and I needed to know what it was.

Preferably before he tried to arrest me.

But wouldn't you know it? We didn't even make it to the car when my phone rang with Marvin's name displayed on the screen.

"What've you got for me?" I asked, turning the screen so Ashley could see who I was talking to. *Normal, Tony, keep acting normal.*

"We found her."

I needed a moment to process what he was saying. "Emily Harris?"

"Yeah. Well, we found what's left of her."

Chapter 27

MARVIN GAVE ME THE location and we set off, but once again the ebb and flow of conversation was missing when we made our way through the quiet streets of the seaside resort. In the height of summer, especially at the weekends, getting around Whitstable is a laborious task. Tourists flock there, favouring it over Herne Bay despite my hometown having a pier and amusements.

On a grey and dreary day in November, the streets were almost empty.

Marvin didn't give me all the details, only that her body had been discovered behind a wheelie bin in the service yard of a restaurant in nearby Seasalter. Lying to the west of Whitstable just like Herne Bay sat a few miles to the east, Seasalter is yet another seaside resort whose heyday was too many decades in the past for most living residents to remember. The pebble beach did nothing to draw the crowds and even the locals would take themselves to Whitstable if they fancied a day sunbathing and swimming.

Emily Harris had never given us reason to believe she would aid the case against Elroy Stewart, but she had been silenced anyway. Was it murder? Probably, but we would have to prove it. Or, rather, someone else would. It wasn't our case, and the call to alert us came only because of her direct involvement in our recent investigation and the fact that she was the prime suspect in the attempt to murder us both last night.

By the time we arrived, the area was cordoned off. A forensic investigation team van was parked against the wall next to the entrance to the service yard and a pair of squad cars had closed off the road. We were waved through and greeted by Chief Inspector Riley when Marvin nudged his arm to point out our arrival.

"Overdose," he stated flatly, "but it looks staged. The coroner will have to confirm it, of course, but if she's a regular heroine user, I'm the pope."

I didn't buy it either. Emily had some issues or perhaps problems was a better term to employ, but I've seen enough drug addicts in my career to know she looked too healthy to be using. That didn't mean she couldn't be a recreational user, but I doubted it. Maybe Rachael Weaver's death was an accident, but this wasn't.

Riley led us into the yard where a white tent was already erected over the body, shielding it from sight and preserving whatever evidence might be lying on or around her.

"Do you want to see her?" Riley asked, his question not about my level of morbid curiosity, but to do with what I might gain from seeing her body.

I shook my head and checked with Ashley. I didn't think there was any benefit to seeing her ruined body. Ashley agreed. All we needed to know was that she had been killed. Elroy undoubtedly had an ironclad alibi for the hours surrounding the time of her death, but we couldn't go near him anyway.

I felt like I was being taunted. Lured to our deaths only to survive by chance, but our survival was likely the reason Emily had to die. Elroy would have known the police would pursue her relentlessly. You don't get to target cops and get away with it. Ultimately, that would have led to her caving under questioning. I had seen the chinks in her armour when we went to her doorstep. Emily knew she had to maintain the lies about how she was injured, but this was so much bigger. If she was caught and didn't point the finger of blame elsewhere, she would have gone down for a long time.

Elroy wasn't willing to risk it.

But I was wrong. DCI Riley had another snippet of information to share with us.

"The anonymous call that sent the fire brigade to Ellison's Electricals last night was made by Emily."

The news stunned me.

Ashley said, "How sure are you?"

Riley pulled a face that said he wasn't one hundred percent, but he said, "Pretty sure. The call was made from a mobile phone registered to her and paid for through her bank account. The tech boys will confirm if it's her voice or not, but I expect to hear that it is. It could be why she was killed."

She was being coerced or blackmailed, but tried to do the right thing. She must have known what Elroy was planning and chose to defy him. It got her killed.

The notion that we were being taunted returned. We couldn't touch Elroy. Heck, we couldn't even go near him. He tried to kill us and then ended the life of the woman whose actions saved our lives.

It was enough to make me forget about Ashley and the impending disaster that is my life.

"We should head back to the nick," Ashley said. "We can't achieve anything here."

I felt tired. Bone weary might be more accurate. The sense of pointlessness had returned, and I wanted to ditch work and skive the way I had been doing for the last few years. Concern for what drove Ashley's questions meant I couldn't entertain such a plan. Instead, I had to stay engaged. At least until I knew whether he really was onto me.

Taking out my car keys, I started back to my car. Ashley followed, saying nothing.

Chapter 28

"I'm not feeling so good," Ashley said once they were on their way back to Herne Bay. To investigate his partner, he first had to lose him. Tony was suspicious already; Ashley could hear it and see it. He'd overplayed his hand with the question about the woman, and it was too late to change that. What he needed now was some time to dig a little deeper.

Busting the Bruce Denton case would crown him in glory. It would earn him recognition and ensure his name was known among the upper echelons. Yet he still struggled to see Tony as the killer. The man wrecked his career trying to solve the case and find the man responsible for Bruce Denton's violent death. Had it really all been so he wouldn't get caught?

Ashley was beginning to feel like a yoyo. One moment he thought he'd uncovered a clue no one else had ever thought to consider. The next he was convinced he had to be wrong and was barking up the wrong tree.

Tony eyed him from the driver's seat, turning a little to look him up and down when they slowed to a stop in traffic.

"You look fine."

"I'm black, Tony. We don't get to look washed out when we feel it." Ashley threw down the race card, trumping any argument his partner might have. Then, because it was the right thing to do in the circumstances and not because he felt genuine regret, he said, "Sorry. The doctors said we needed to watch for any strange symptoms. I guess ... I don't know how to describe it other than to say I just don't feel right."

Ashley could see Tony regarding him sceptically, but he didn't argue.

"Are you going home then?"

Thankful it had worked, Ashley planned to do anything other than go home. The moment he left the Herne Bay nick and could move freely, he was going to call Bruce Denton's fiancée. He had a couple of questions for her and wanted to ask them without Tony around to hear. Then he would rerun the VRN check, and while that compiled, he would trawl through social media looking for something that would confirm his worst fears. It would either be there, or it wouldn't. What he did after that would be determined by what he could find.

With a nod, Ashley said, "Yeah. Sorry to abandon you. I can work from home though. I'll go back over the list of cases and find one for us to start on tomorrow."

"Not planning to see a doctor then?"

The question made Ashley pause. He hadn't considered how his claim to be suffering lingering effects from the fire might make a plan to just work from home sound blasé.

"Um, yeah, that's a good point," he managed to find some words to deflect his partner, but the tone Tony employed made it clear he wasn't entirely convinced Ashley felt too ill to work. "Maybe I should swing by the hospital and get checked out."

Tony nodded and Ashley saw from the confident look on his face that he'd just walked into a trap.

"I'll take you. It's safer than letting you drive yourself. One of the biggest concerns they had was lung inflammation leading to shortness of breath. No good you losing consciousness at the wheel."

Ashley cursed himself for not thinking far enough ahead, but how was he going to get around it now? He knew he had to reply with thanks. It was no good saying he would be all right, not when they were talking about public safety.

Tony's phone rang, cutting through the tension in the car like an alarm going off. He was driving, both hands on the wheel, but even though it's against the law to handle your phone while driving, that's precisely what he did.

For long enough to see whose name was on the screen.

Tossing it sideways for Ashley to catch, he returned his focus to the road ahead. "It's Cindy. Rachael Weaver's daughter."

Ashley almost said, "I wonder what she wants," but to do so would be redundant so he jabbed the green button to answer the call and put it to his ear. "This is Detective Sergeant Long. Detective Sergeant Heaton is driving."

"Put it on speaker, won't you?" said Tony, making it clear he thought that was an obvious thing to do.

"Get a hands-free kit installed," Ashley shot back, hitting the speaker button anyway.

"Um," said Cindy Gunderson. "Sorry, are you the guys who were at my mum's house two days ago? Sorry, I don't remember your names, and I lost the card the older guy gave me."

"Older guy?" mouthed Tony, feigning insult and forgetting the deep-running suspicion between he and Ashley for a moment of levity.

"Sorry," Cindy said again. "I should have said that my mum is Rachael Weaver."

"We know who you are, Mrs Gunderson," said Ashley, holding the phone in the air. "What can we do for you?"

"I think it's more a case of what I can do for you. I contacted mum's solicitor yesterday, to let them know she had died and to start all the paperwork and things that have to happen now. They said they had a letter for me and sent someone around with it this morning."

"They hand delivered it?" Tony questioned.

Ashley, his immediate reaction to question where this was going, had put two and two together and was now staring at Tony with wild eyes.

"Yes, but that's not important," said Cindy. "The letter is from my mum and while it's addressed to me, it's really for you."

Tony's eyebrows danced above his eyes. He hadn't made the leap yet and Ashley debated whether he would prove to be way off the mark with his guess.

He wasn't.

"The letter is a complete confession. Mum lied when she withdrew her statement and says that she was coerced or rather threatened into doing so. There's lots of details with names and more. I'm guessing this is something you want to see?"

Tony didn't answer the question. Instead he asked, "Where are you?"

Chapter 29

WE MADE NO MISTAKE this time. Ashley missed his chance to get the promised truth from Rachael Weaver when he acquiesced to Cindy's demand to leave her cancer-ridden mother alone until the following morning. A morning that never came.

I could have harassed him about how he suddenly seemed to be over whatever ailment was bothering him, but I wasn't sure how I wanted to play things yet. On the one hand it might serve me well to have him elsewhere. That way I could move freely and make some calls to hopefully find out who he'd been speaking to. Something had changed in the last thirty-six hours. A day and a half ago I was making sure he got out of a burning building. When the firefighters told him what I had done, he expressed his deep-felt gratitude. Since then he'd learned something, or perhaps just figured it out - I always said he was a smart cookie - but whatever the case, every facet of his behaviour was different.

Chewing over what my next move should be during the journey to Cindy's house in Herne Bay, I had drawn no conclusion by the time we got to her door. She was expecting us and opened it as we were walking down the garden path.

The letter was in her hand.

Knowing it might prove to be a vital piece of evidence, I donned a pair of gloves. Ashley did the same and we all went to her kitchen where she placed the letter and its envelope on a central island. She lived in an average semi-detached house, but one with a big garden that backed onto scrubland. A single-storey extension to the back of the house permitted a far larger kitchen and dining space than the original design intended. It was light and airy and made me wish I had the money to do the same with my house.

I noted all these things in the seconds I required to dig out my reading glasses. Ashley was next to me, close enough that I could hear the slight rasp the smoke had left in his lungs. The doctors assured us it would pass in a few days or a few weeks. I think it worried Ashley, but I had far bigger concerns to fill my fear quota.

The letter was handwritten and addressed to Cindy just as she claimed. There was no postage stamp on the envelope, but beneath her daughter's name, Rachael had recorded her instructions: To be hand delivered to my daughter upon my death. Should I somehow survive her, this letter is to be hand delivered directly to the most senior police officer at Whitstable Police Station.

While I inspected the envelope and used a finger to lever it open to be sure there was nothing left hidden inside, Ashley reached the bottom of the first page and passed it to me. He moved onto the next page – from what I could see there were four in total – and I got started on the meat of it.

It was precisely as Cindy described: a complete confession in which her mother stated that Elroy Stewart *was* the man in the silver BMW. She identified him in an identity parade, which more and more people (and cops) choose to call a lineup due to the proliferation of America TV shows. She subsequently withdrew her statement when men came to her house that night to threaten her. Rachael made it clear that she wanted to stand up to them and had initially done so, refusing to go back to the police to say that she had it wrong, but she awoke the next day to the sound of something being posted through her letterbox. It was photographs of Cindy and her children. They knew where she lived and where Rachael's grandchildren went to school. The pictures didn't come with a note, but the threat was obvious, and she caved.

She was thoroughly ashamed that she hadn't been braver, but while I was overjoyed to hold evidence in my hand that would alter the entire case against Elroy Stewart, there was more to learn.

Rachael claimed that they watched her for weeks. She would walk to the shops or to her job, or to go to collect her grandkids from school. She admitted becoming paranoid. Additionally, she said the threats and stalking manifested as racism and claimed she had never before felt any animosity toward anyone of a different race prior to being targeted. However, she soon saw all black men as criminals and questioned if the feeling would ever pass.

Over time, she moved on, but she never forgot about it. The date at the top of the letter was less than five years ago. She'd written it in the summer. When I questioned Cindy about that, she said it was just after her mum was first diagnosed with cancer. The sickness had prompted Rachael to consider her mortality. The letter came as a result.

On page three, Rachael provided descriptions for the three men who had come to her door the very first time. She was even able to name one, Bobby Lamson, and went on to explain how she came to discover his name. Chance placed her in the right place at the wrong time, as it were. But sitting in the corner of the Ancient Mariner public house with a friend one afternoon many years after Daniel Mahony's murder, he came in with a woman. She recognised him immediately and froze, memories of the terror she felt returning like a bucket of icy water down her spine.

Her friend asked what was bothering her, but she didn't reveal the truth. Unable to get up for fear her legs might not support her, such was her terror the man at the bar might recognise her as she recognised him, she listened.

Seeing Rachael staring, her friend, who remained unnamed in the letter, asked if she knew Bobby. Startled, Rachael merely said that he looked familiar and had to hush her companion when she almost called him over. Though she only knew Bobby in passing, it was through his grandmother, so she knew his last name too.

I read to the end of the last page and gave myself a moment to think.

It seemed as though we had him. Elroy that is, though there was enough to warrant arresting Bobby too. But the letter – a confession from beyond the grave – wouldn't be enough to convince the crown prosecution service to let us charge anyone, even though it was a big leap forward. Taken at face value, which is to say before a defence lawyer ripped it to shreds, it put Elroy Stewart behind the wheel of a car that had just been used in a hit and run incident that took a man's life. It also fingered Bobby Lamson as a willing accomplice, leaning on at least one of the star witnesses while Elroy was in custody.

It wasn't enough by itself, but we could pick up Bobby and turn the screw, so to speak, until he revealed something.

Taking me to one side, as if the invisible barrier that had sprung up between us wasn't there, Ashley whispered, "I'm not getting involved, Tony. There was no ambiguity in the order from Superintendent Charters, and my boss backed it up. We have to hand this over."

"Stuff that," I scoffed. "Elroy Stewart killed Daniel Mahony. He's intimidated witnesses, coerced Emily Harris into lying to get that bogus charge against you and has to be behind her murder. He's so guilty it's hard to believe there isn't a line of cops waiting to arrest him. To hell with the rules and what our bosses demand. We can nail him. If we can find one more piece of evidence or one more statement that calls his alibis into question, they will have to acknowledge that we were right to keep going."

Ashley wanted to nick Elroy and so he should. He'd brought about the first black mark on the young detective's otherwise blemish-free record. He could erase it by proving he was behind Daniel Mahony's murder, but he knew as well as I did that we were going to be on dodgy ground until we had what we needed.

Sensing his wavering spirit, I said, "We can do the questioning at Whitstable nick."

Chapter 30

WE TOOK CINDY WITH us, insisting she had to record a statement for the chain of evidence even though we would still have to corroborate with the solicitors who held the letter for the last five years that it was Rachael Weaver who gave it to them.

The one joy of being assigned to the cold case taskforce, even though I still thought the whole exercise was nothing more than the chief constable covering his butt, was that we could go anywhere and request an interview room to use. That worked doubly in Whitstable because the crime we were investigating happened there.

Marvin the Martian was still out or had returned to the nick only to go out again. Dealing with Emily's body wouldn't have taken this long, but I didn't enquire as to his whereabouts. Leaving Ashley to request an interview room, I led Cindy through the nick to make myself a cup of tea and offer her one.

Yet again, the day I thought I was going to have had taken a sideways turn.

"Will this take long?" she asked, trying hard not to sound like it was a big inconvenience.

"Half an hour," I fired back while filling a kettle. "Maybe a little more. Thank you for doing this. Your mother's testimony will be vitally important to a case against a very bad man. Getting criminals off the street is what people expect us to do, but it's never as easy as they make it look on TV."

"I'm sure it isn't," Cindy replied.

We were making small talk to kill time, but I had barely made the teas when Ashley appeared to say he was ready.

We recorded Cindy's statement, going back over the points we covered at her house to make sure we had it all. Confirming the facts with the solicitors was a task for later; it wasn't all that important. Not when compared with picking up Bobby Lamson.

Cindy was happy to be able to get back to her day, but also content to have done the right thing. Her mother was going to put a killer behind bars – that's how she saw it, and I didn't disagree.

While I showed her out, Ashley visited the dispatch office. We would arrest Bobby ourselves if we could, but neither one of us wanted to spend the day trawling around trying to find him. His face was in the system, naturally, so by the time I rejoined him, every officer on duty in Whitstable and for miles around knew to be on the lookout for him.

The duty sergeant asked if we wanted a unit to go to his address, but we kept that task for ourselves. It was the one place we hoped to be able to find him. Criminals don't keep regular hours, and it was still morning, so the chances of catching him at home were high. We both wanted to see how Bobby reacted when he realised we were going to arrest him. People cannot hide their initial reaction, no one is that good unless they are prepared. I doubted he would be and without wanting to be unkind, Bobby didn't come across as the sharpest knife in the drawer.

So the chance to see his eyes when we slapped on the cuffs might help to guide the strategy for when we interviewed him. He was guilty and if we could build a good enough case he would do a stint inside. So far all we had was threatening behaviour twenty years ago. I wanted him for his part in keeping Elroy out of jail. For that he would do some hard time.

"Ready?" I asked Ashley. It was time to see if we could find Mr Lamson. My partner was either feeling better or had been faking his under-the-weatherness earlier for there was no sign of it now and he hadn't mentioned it in more than an hour.

"I'm going to the gents before we head out," he announced. It reminded me that I ought to do the same. He was already leaving the dispatch office, and I was about to follow when I saw that he'd put his things down.

Including his phone.

And the screen hadn't timed out yet. I needed to pee, but it was going to have to wait.

I snatched it up before the screen went blank and would require his face to unlock it. If I lifted my head to look about, checking to make sure no one had seen what I was doing, it would draw attention to what I was doing. Instead, I kept my head down and opened his text message app. The phone was the same as mine, although Ashley's was a newer model. That was good because I can barely operate my own device and would be hopeless with a different make.

There were texts between him and Tanya which I ignored to check the content of the messages between the names I didn't know. Flicking my eyes over them at speed, I couldn't find any that contained my name. In fact, they were all innocent and boring. His grandmother was about to turn eighty and the family was organising a big get together.

Guiltily glancing down the hallway outside, I told myself I would hear him returning. I knew it was true, but the knowledge did nothing to calm my speeding pulse. Closing the message app, I opened his call log.

There were a bunch of names listed, but I ignored everything before two days ago. Whatever caused the change in him happened yesterday.

"Excuse me," said a voice that damned near made me wet myself. For a half second I thought one of the officers working the dispatch desk felt inclined to question what I was doing with Ashley's phone, but she merely wanted to leave the room. I was blocking the way.

I moved to one side to let her go by and waited for my heart to restart.

Certain I had only seconds remaining before my partner returned, I looked at his phone screen again. Most of the calls had names assigned to them – they were people he knew. But there was one that was just a number. He called it once yesterday afternoon for a call that lasted almost ten minutes.

Heart in my mouth, I touched the number to redial it and held the phone to my ear.

It rang.

I heard a door open in the hallway and a pair of feet coming my way. It had to be Ashley. My pulse hammered, my heart beating triple time. I was moments from being caught. My hands were sweaty, my fingers slick as I continued to hold the phone to my ear.

The footsteps were getting closer.

"Bryan Hayworth." The voice resounded in my ear clear and confident, the person at the other end of the line not recognising the number and answering by identifying themselves. I do the same thing.

Ripping the phone away from my head, I ended the call with a vicious jab of my index finger and grabbed the rest of Ashley's things just as he came around the corner. Masking my activities by making it look as though I was impatient to get moving, I thrust his coat and bag into his arms, forcing him to grab them, then placed his phone on top.

Was Bryan about to call back or would he assume Ashley butt dialled him? My heart continued to jackhammer in my chest as I waited for it to start ringing. I had no clue what I would say to explain how his phone had made the call other than to deny all knowledge and say it must have happened when he put it down.

"Ready to go?" Ashley enquired, one eyebrow raised to leave no doubt he was questioning my sense of urgency.

"I want to be the one to pick up Bobby. You know we could actually crack this case." I played into his fantasy. With so many older relatives in senior positions, he had family pressure to perform. His, or more accurately our, recent successes would have them all talking about him, but you're only ever as good as your next case. Scoring another big win wasn't just something he wanted. He yearned for it.

"Okay, Tony, let's go get Bobby Lamson."

Chapter 31

IN THE CAR MY mind raced. Bryan Hayworth hated me. He hadn't at first. In fact, when I started at the nick as a young detective, he took me under his wing and helped me. Even when it became clear I was going places and aced the sergeants' exam, he remained friendly enough though the desire to help me waned.

However, when I fought against his suggestion that Bruce Denton might have been killed by a cop, the tide turned. I never got the sense that he suspected me. But his view was unpopular, and I used that to turn everyone against him. I hadn't set out to have him shunned, but when the whispers grew, I saw my opportunity. All I wanted was to shut him up, but he became a pariah and ended up leaving the nick.

And now Ashley was talking to him.

I could only imagine what he might have said but could be certain it was all negative when it came to me. Had he spent the last thirty years trying to piece together who might have killed

Bruce Denton? None of the people associated with the case; Bruce's family, friends, and relatives, ever once suggested they had been contacted by another detective. I didn't think he'd been poking around, but I couldn't be sure. If he suspected me, did he have a file of information he'd gathered over the years?

I couldn't get my pulse to settle and I was sweating. My armpits were swamps, the cotton of my shirt soaked where my body willingly betrayed me. My jacket covered it, but I could feel the perspiration on my face and neck.

If Ashley had noticed – how could he not? – then he was choosing to say nothing and that worried me just as much. What did he know? Had he figured out the car thing? Had he already rerun the VRN check?

"Tony?" his voice cut through my thoughts.

I glanced over at him.

"You missed the turning."

I was so caught up inside my own head I had fallen into some kind of autopilot mode. I'm not sure where we might have ended up if he hadn't spoken, but it wouldn't have been Bobby Lamson's house. Flicking my eyes to the rear-view mirror, I checked behind me, turned on my indicator and performed a U-turn when there was space.

"I've been trying to figure out what line we can take with him," I lied. "He's been lying to give Elroy an alibi for so long now I'm wondering how we can make him crack."

"Chances are he'll lawyer up the moment we arrest him."

He was probably right about that. We both doubted the letter would be enough to secure a conviction, but that was no reason not to question him. One never knows what little nugget of information might slip out.

Pulling up to his grandmother's house, I saw the curtain twitch. She was unpleasant the first time we met her and wouldn't be any different today. It's a little sad to admit, but I liked that we were going to ruin her day. Bobby's sleek black Mercedes was parked in the street, suggesting he was home. Just as I expected.

We were about to find out.

Chapter 32

ASHLEY PRAYED BOBBY WAS at home. Sure, the letter from Mrs Weaver was a breakthrough. A big one potentially, even if it wouldn't be enough by itself. Yet he couldn't convince his brain to focus on the Daniel Mahony case.

Tony was acting strange and there was no mistaking his nervousness. He'd never seen him so tightly wound. The vein in Tony's neck pulsed visibly each time his heart beat and it was doing that far faster than it ought to be. They were back on the trail of Elroy Stewart and that was good, but Ashley couldn't shift the sense that his partner was using the case to deflect attention away from Bruce Denton.

He had to go through with the search for Bobby Lamson now, there was no alternative, but the moment he could get away, he would be looking at Tony's old case with a new set of eyes. He hoped he was wrong, but more and more he could see how the old detective could be the killer. Next time, when he looked at the evidence, he would do so with that in mind and it's always easier to figure things out if you already know who carries the guilt.

Chapter 33

THE FRONT DOOR OPENED before we could get to it, Bobby's grandmother firing a scowl in our direction.

I asked, "Is he in?"

"Go away. You're not wanted here. This is harassment."

"No, this is arrest," I corrected her, fighting to keep the smile from my face. "Your grandson is guilty of intimidation, threatening a person with physical harm, and providing false alibi. Step aside, Mrs Lamson."

I was going in whether she stepped out of the way or not. Not that I was going to treat her roughly, but I would move her to one side if she continued to bar my way.

A door slammed open at the back of the house.

"He's running!" I yelled, barging past the old lady before she could move.

"Hey!" she yelled, following her cry of shock with a tirade of expletives.

With the air turning blue behind me, I ran through the house. Three strides carried me past the staircase and into the kitchen. Another three took me to the open backdoor.

I heard Ashley shout, "I'm going around!" but I didn't hold much hope he would be able to catch our runner. His limp was less noticeable today, but it was still there. Maybe he could run if he ignored the pain, but he wasn't about to sprint. He would be better off in the car where he could easily outpace anyone on foot, but the keys were in my pocket.

Exiting the rear of the house into a small back garden, I was surprised to find how well-tended it was. Is it judgemental to admit I expected to find nothing but weeds and litter? Three-foot-high brick walls ran down both sides to a six-foot wall at the back. In it, a tall wooden gate hung open where Bobby went through too fast to think about closing it behind him. I could hear him thrashing through the overgrowth in his bid to get away.

He's younger than me by most of a decade, but far from fit. Not that I'm claiming to be a regular gym goer, but the size of Bobby's belly gave me reason to think I might catch him. With that in mind, I burst through the gate, turned hard left and put my head down.

The thing with old towns like Whitstable is that they were built long before the concept of a car came along. All they had back then were horses and carts. Cheap houses were built in long lines, all attached to one another with the next row erected so the backs faced each other. An alleyway was left to separate the tiny gardens, but where in my youth these passages were in semi-regular use, modern kids didn't play outside the way we did in the seventies and eighties. The space between the walls was narrow enough to start with, but thick brambles, car batteries, bags of rubbish, dog mess, and more combined to make the alley almost impenetrable. I felt like I ought to be swinging a machete like a soldier in the jungle.

Some forty yards ahead of me, Bobby was having the same fight. I could both see and hear him. If I could just keep moving, I would catch him, but the slower he went, the more chance there was that Ashley would be in place to cut him off.

A bramble snagged at my face, the long, thick tendril hanging down to block my path. It caught the skin on my left cheek, undoubtedly leaving a mark. I slapped it aside and pushed on. Abruptly, the overgrowth stopped. One of the homeowners was conscientious enough to have cut it all back. It was like running through soup only to suddenly break free. I shot forward, but only until the greenery closed in again.

Sidestepping a black sack with rubbish spilling from a hole in the side, I realised Bobby was no longer ahead of me. I pushed on, a flash of fear making me question if he was hidden in an alcove and about to jump out on me. I slowed my pace, looking for signs of danger and finding none.

Was he there? The overgrown and dark alley certainly provided enough hiding places. He could have ducked through a back gate and be waiting with a knife for all I knew. Wouldn't that be a way to go with less than two weeks until retirement. It sounded like a cliché from a bad cop movie.

I had covered less than fifty yards, but my breath was ragged and my lungs protested. Ashley would have called for backup the moment I took off so uniformed officers in squad cars were inbound. They would seal off the area, but that didn't mean we would find Bobby anytime soon. He would not only know the area, but the people living here were all his neighbours. Was he already in someone else's house, hunkered down and invisible? Going door to door to search and find him would take hours and demand multiple officers. We could justify it, but maybe it would be better to withdraw and give him time to resurface.

The blow caught me by surprise even though I told myself to be ready for it. It wasn't a punch or a kick, but a two-handed shove. Bobby came at me from behind, knocking me to the ground. I sprawled in the dirt, my face landing inches from a pile of unspeakableness that had once resided inside a dog's back end. A shadow blocked out the light when Bobby leapt over me to continue running.

Damp, cold, muddy, and angry, I snarled with rage and threw myself back into the chase. I didn't bother shouting for him to stop. That's what we are supposed to do. It's in the manual and every cop gets trained to do it the same way. If we don't identify ourselves, a suspect might argue that they thought the cop chasing them was an assailant who intended them harm. But listen, no one ever stops when you tell them to. No one. Ever. And I was already out of breath.

If they put me on a stand and asked me under oath if I shouted for Bobby to stop, I would lie. Happily, and with a clear conscience.

The undergrowth retreated again, widening the space so we could actually run. He got there first, just a few yards ahead of me and the gap between us widened.

Finding my voice at last, I shouted, "Give it up, Bobby. Can't you hear the sirens?"

They had just reached my ears, the blissful sound of backup arriving. I made out two separate sirens, both converging on our general location. They wouldn't see us, hidden in the alleyway as we were, but my shouts would draw them.

Barely able to fill my lungs with enough air to keep my body moving, I nevertheless bellowed so Ashley and whoever else was here would know which way to go.

Bobby cut right, turning into a new alley that ran between two houses. Ahead of us, the alley met the street, and we would be in the open. I prayed there would be a squad car out there somewhere ready to pounce. But I was catching him.

Desperation showed on his face when he glanced over his shoulder to see how close I was. Running was the wrong thing to do. It made him look guilty for a start, but he'd thought he might be able to get away.

He shot from the end of the alley and had to bank hard to the left to avoid running into the side of a parked car. It forced him to slow and that was all I needed to get close enough to tackle him. He was about beaten anyway, not that I was doing much better, but a lunge and a shove proved enough to finish him.

Bobby clipped the rear quarter of the car, leaving a dent where his knee struck a panel. I heard a grunt of pain as he tumbled and spun. His torso hit the boot of the car behind that and he bounced off, losing his footing. Out of control, he fell to the tarmac between the two cars.

I could have followed him down, heroically snapping the cuffs on his wrists, but it was about all I could do not to collapse.

There was no oxygen left in my body, and I was certain I had a piece of lung hanging out of my mouth.

The uniforms were coming. I caught sight of them from the corner of my eye as I came out of the alley. Typically, they had been facing the wrong way, but they were running to get to me now, showing off their youthful vigour.

"Bobby Lamson," I coughed and choked between ragged breaths, "I am arresting you for being fat, ugly, and stupid."

His face, covered in spittle and sweat, registered confusion.

"Only joking," I conceded, and proceeded to read his rights correctly. Truly impressed I had run a suspect to ground, even if he was overweight and even more unfit than me, I took a moment to bask in my own glory.

The young cops arrived, two men in their twenties out of Whitstable nick. I didn't recognise them, but they knew who I was. One even said, "Good take," to compliment me, though I suspect it was mostly due to being impressed an old guy like me could still run.

Ashley arrived as they were peeling him off the ground. He was a little out of breath and limping worse than before.

"What kept you?" I joked, still trying to get my own breathing under control.

Ignoring my question, Ashley asked, "Did he resist?"

"He was good enough to assault me, yes." His solicitor would argue the letter was inadmissible as evidence since the person who wrote it – which we would have to prove was indeed Rachael Weaver – was no longer around. That no longer mattered because the fool had assaulted a police officer.

Bobby blurted, "What? I never hit you!"

"You threw me to the ground," I wafted a hand at my clothes. "That's assault, Bobby, and it's the least of your worries."

Constable Barry, his last name not his first, asked, "Okay for us to take him?" They had introduced themselves once they had Bobby restrained. Constable Field went back for their squad car and was with it now, waiting to load my suspect.

"Yes, thank you, chaps. Take him to your nick. We'll be along shortly."

They took him away, people in the street watching from their doorsteps or from behind their net curtains. Most of them wandered back inside once the squad car pulled away. My car was still in the next street and thankfully the keys for it hadn't escaped my pocket during the chase. In no hurry, and wishing my lungs didn't hurt from the unusual level of exertion, I took the long way around rather than back through the alley, with Ashley walking by my side.

I wanted to ask him about Bryan Hayworth. I yearned to know what he thought he knew about the woman in the video. But I said nothing. The day was ticking by and I was yet to figure out what my next move could be.

Chapter 34

ASHLEY GOT OUT OF the car the moment Tony parked it. The next task on their list was to interview Bobby, but he would have to be processed first and if he then demanded a lawyer, which he almost certainly would – savvy career criminal that he is – it could be hours before they could start. That meant he had time to investigate his partner.

The very thought drove a chill through him. Cops are all about the brotherhood. His father, uncles, and cousins all talked about honour and loyalty as though they were immutable. To turn against your fellow law enforcement officer, let alone your partner, was a cardinal sin.

Unless they were guilty.

There is nothing worse than a cop who turns to crime. Dirty cops, the ones on the take who turn a blind eye to crimes so they can make a buck, are worse than the criminals themselves. Ashley didn't see Tony in that category, but he worried he might be someone who felt he had reason to take the law into his own hands. That wasn't as bad, but it wasn't any better either. Ashley could imagine the discussion at his father's table. Where should the line be drawn? They were responsible for upholding the law yet at the same time the system was stacked against them.

Ashley would always argue that the line could never be crossed. A cop had to stay on the right side of it at all times, but this was different.

He was talking about murder.

But he had to be sure. To accuse Tony only to be proven wrong would put a black stain on him he might never rub off. It would undo all the good work he had done and jeopardise his future. So, above all else, he had to be absolutely certain before he pointed the finger.

Turning around to walk backwards while Tony was still getting out of his car, Ashley said, "I'm still not feeling right. I'm going to find somewhere quiet to work. Let me know when the suspect is ready for interview, okay?"

Tony looked at him over the roof of the car, his face hard to read. Did he buy it? When his partner gave him a thumbs up, Ashley chose not to question it.

Heading inside the nick, he took out his phone. The first task on his list would be to call Bruce Denton's former fiancée. He had her number already and just had to hope she would answer. Rather than grab a desk in the pool room where the detectives worked, he aimed for one of the incident rooms. He knew from recent visits that at least one remained unused, and it still was when he got to it.

Tucked away from everyone else he could dig into a fellow officer's life without fear of being caught.

He needed his laptop to find the number for Angela Maddox. Formerly Angela Wilcox, he hadn't needed to dig very far to find her number. It was also in Tony's secret case notes, but it looked as though he'd stopped contacting her many years ago. For some of the people closest to Bruce, most notably his neighbours, Tony had been back time and again, at least once a year, to check what they could remember. There were notes next to their names and dates to show when he last visited.

For some, like Bruce's parents, the dates stopped. It coincided with their deaths and there were fewer and fewer people left to speak with about the case. Angela was one of them, but she and Bruce were no longer together when he died. It ought to mean she would know nothing, but what Ashley wanted to ask wasn't about Bruce's murder.

Opening his phone app, he was about to tap the icon to bring up the number pad when he spotted the most recent call. It was one he hadn't made.

Had he pocket dialled it? It took him a second to figure out whose number it was. The call lasted four seconds and was outgoing from his phone, not incoming from Bryan's. Chewing his bottom lip as he thought, Ashley tried to work the timings in his head.

It would have been right around when they were leaving the station to look for Bobby Lamson. The truth hit him like a hammer to the chest. He hadn't made the call, but Tony had. It was a leap to say the least. Tony wouldn't have been able to unlock the phone. Shouldn't have been able to, anyway. And why would he make the call?

Ashley recalled that he left his phone in the dispatch room when he ran to the gents. It meant Tony had opportunity, but what would make him think to check his call log and dial an unlisted contact? Bryan made it abundantly clear he and Tony were anything but friends so it wasn't as though Tony would recognise the number.

Perplexed, Ashley thumbed the number to redial it.

Bryan picked up after two rings.

"It's Ashley Long again. Did I call you this morning?"

"Yeah, but when I answered there was no one there and the line went dead a moment later. When you didn't call back, I figured you called by accident."

"There was no one there?" Ashley pushed to confirm. "No one said anything?"

"No. Was there something you needed?"

If he had pocket dialled the number he would have heard Bryan's muffled voice in his pocket and having done it by accident, assuming he couldn't hear it for whatever reason, the call would have lasted longer.

"Did you end the call or did I?"

"You did. Like I said, I figured you hit the call button by accident. I do that sometimes."

Everyone does that sometimes, but this wasn't that. Ashley thanked Bryan and ended the call. Tony had not only been checking his phone, he'd figured out how to unlock it without needing Ashley's face. It was disturbing.

But also telling.

Feeling weary and very much alone, Ashley settled into a chair and typed Angela's number into his phone. Now fifty-five years old, she worked for a pharmaceutical company in Bagshot in Berkshire. It was probably the wrong time of the day to call her, and when she failed to answer her mobile, he dialled the number on the firm's website.

A well-spoken receptionist answered.

"This is Detective Sergeant Long of the Kent Police. I need to speak with Angela Maddox. Is she in the office today?"

"One moment, please." Ashley's ear filled with 'hold' music though he wasn't sure if he was holding while being transferred or whether the receptionist lady was checking if Angela was in or not.

"Angela Maddox." The voice had a nasal quality to it as though the owner was suffering from a cold.

Ashley introduced himself and asked, "I am speaking to Angela Maddox, yes?"

"This is she. Have I done something wrong?"

"Not that I know of, Mrs Maddox. I wish to speak with you about Bruce Denton."

The line went quiet. The sort of quiet you can only get when the person at the other end has stopped breathing.

"Angela?"

"Yes, sorry," she replied, her voice now distant and thoughtful. "I'm sorry. I never thought I would hear anyone say his name again. I haven't heard it spoken aloud in years."

Sensing a need to take delicate steps, Ashley said, "I apologise if this stirs up old memories. There is new evidence, and I need to ask you a few questions."

"New evidence? You think you might catch his killer?"

Knowing better than to commit to an answer, he deflected. "I want to ask you about his relationships after you split up. Did your engagement end because he met someone else?" Ashley didn't really know where he was going with his line of questioning and couldn't easily say what he hoped to find out. It linked back to the woman in the video and what role she played in Bruce's murder.

"We split up because he was cheating on me."

"So there was someone else. Do you know who it was?"

"Not someone else, Detective. Lots of someones."

He could have corrected her about his rank but let it go. It wasn't important. "You're saying he was a serial cheat? That he had lots of women on the go?"

"Precisely that. I was young then and stupidly expected him to be faithful to me. Trust me, I've since learned that all men will shag anything that gets close enough."

Ashley knew that wasn't true, but yet again kept his mouth shut.

"Can you name any of the women he dated while you were with him or in the period after you split up?"

"No, sorry. I don't think I ever knew, but if I did that information left my head a long time ago. I thought I loved Bruce and was ready to marry him. You could say I had a lucky escape. He didn't deserve what happened to him, but I had nothing to do with it."

"No, I'm sure you didn't, Mrs Maddox. That's not even a question I want to ask. Can I ask how you found out he was cheating?"

"He came home with scratches on his body. That was the first time I suspected him, but he told me he'd been in a fight. He was out with some friends. At least that's what he told me, though I never really believed him. I started to look for signs and marked

237

the box of condoms in his drawer. They were going down faster than we were having sex. I took that as a fairly good indicator he was getting it elsewhere but before I could confront him, two women attacked him in the street. He'd got one of them drunk and slept with her. They were both angry about it."

Ashley interrupted, "You mean like he took advantage of her? Raped her?"

"Oh, I don't know about that. No one used the word 'rape'." The question had shocked her. "But it was obvious he'd slept with her. I didn't need any further proof. It was a Saturday morning, and we were on Herne Bay High Street. I took my engagement ring off, threw it at him, and walked away. He asked me to marry him, but didn't want me to move in until we were married, even though we were sleeping together, and he wouldn't set a date. It took me a while to figure out why, but like I said, in many ways I had a lucky escape. Better to get out early than to have to get divorced. Which happened with the next guy when I caught him cheating with his twenty-two-year-old secretary."

Ashley didn't need to hear any more. He certainly didn't want to know about Angela's other failed relationships. Bruce was a womaniser who would stoop low enough to take advantage of a woman when she'd had too much to drink. If the woman in the video was Tony's wife, was she having an affair?

Or was it something else?

Chapter 35

ASHLEY TAKING HIMSELF OFF to work alone helped me, not that I believed his claim to be feeling 'off' again. I knew, or at least suspected, he would be checking into me, but for the life of me couldn't think what there was that I could do about it.

There wasn't any evidence to tie me to the crime. I made sure of that thirty years ago by being super prepared. The video almost caught me out which was why I threw it in a bog. I could see it was Mary, but no one had come forward to identify her. That's not to say no one came forward, but we had everything from, 'It might be my gran,' to, 'That's definitely Karen Carpenter'.

If there had been a call to identify my wife I would know about it. Unless it went straight to Ashley, but again I couldn't figure out how that would happen. Not that it mattered. He was onto me and because I believed that, I needed to be ready to act. If he dug deep enough he would find the VRN and connect it to

Mary. That would lead him to figure out she was the woman in the video, which had to be what he already suspected.

That would lead him to me.

I could argue that it wasn't her and maybe they wouldn't be able to prove it, but once they shone the searchlight in my direction the evidence would mount. No matter which way I looked at it, Ashley was the problem. The longer he spent digging into the past, the more likely it was that he would uncover the truth. My anxious gut cried out that he was already too close.

I already knew in my heart I was going to have to deal with him. It was that or run away and hope we could stay ahead of whatever authorities they sent after us. Neither option was palatable. Life on the run or murder again.

It helped that I had already been investigated when Ashley was knocked down outside his house. It would make a second investigation problematic for DI Griffiths. The key, though, was to make sure there was no reason to suspect me in the first place.

Unable to get my heart to stop beating double time, I took out my phone. My fingers were shaking. Nervously, I typed out a text. '*Mary, I don't want you to panic, but please have the bags ready. I think Ashley is getting closer. We may have to run. Delete this message as soon as you have read it!*'

It was a terrifying scenario we had talked about many times in the past. I doubted running away would work, but we both agreed that if it came to it, we wanted to try. I know how facial recognition works and could disguise both of us sufficiently with wigs, sunglasses and hats, that getting spotted was unlikely. The car we would use wasn't registered to either of our names, but it was in the longer-term task of evading capture that we would come unstuck. We had some money put away, but I would need fake identification and new credits cards if we were to succeed and I had none of those things.

Maybe we could find some cash-in-hand work and survive like that for a while, but a new life in the sun somewhere would be marred by eternally looking over our shoulders. Whichever way I looked at it, eliminating Ashley was the only sensible option.

I felt sick.

Forcing myself to analyse my situation calmly – trust me, that wasn't easy to do – my first thought was that I needed to know more. More than anything else, my panic was due to the knowledge vacuum in which I operated. Did Ashley really know anything or not? What had he discussed with Bryan Hayworth? How the heck could I get answers to my questions without asking Ashley?

A possible solution presented itself almost instantly, but it was one that filled me with fear. If he was anything like me, Ashley would talk to his fiancée about work. Probably in general terms, but there was a distinct possibility he told Tanya about his conversation with Bryan.

I thought for a minute, pressuring my beleaguered brain to devise a strategy that might get her to reveal what I wanted to know. After a few minutes I gave up and simply dialled her number. I had taken it from Ashley weeks ago, not long after we had our first dice with death. Well, I suppose it was me who did the dicing when DS Glenn Beckett tried to shoot a hole in my head. Regardless, I had her number and was calling it.

I didn't know where Ashley had gone but his car was still outside – I could see it through the window – so feeling weak from the adrenaline that refused to stop coursing through my bloodstream, I found a quiet spot near the exit and waited for Tanya to answer.

When she did I started talking. "Tanya, hi, this is Tony Heaton. Ashley's old git of a partner." I kept my tone light and friendly and wondered if Ashley might have told her about his suspicions.

"Is he okay?" she asked, her words urgent and concerned.

"Oh, goodness, yes. Sorry, I didn't mean to make you worry." It hadn't occurred to me that my call might make her think he was hurt.

She breathed a sigh of relief and the next time she spoke her voice was neutral and businesslike.

"Is there something I can help you with?"

Now I had to choose my words with care. "I'm a little worried about him, that's all. He's ... ah, do you think he's working too hard?" I wanted to come across as concerned about him before I probed her about what he got up to yesterday.

Tanya made a 'Hmmming' sound and I wondered what she was going to say in response. My nerves, which were already shot, insisted I had just made a huge error. She was going to end the call quickly and immediately phone Ashley to report my fake concern.

"Thank you for calling, Tony," she said. "This has been bothering me for a while and I'm glad to hear it's not just me."

It was my turn to breathe a sigh a relief though mine was more like a full body shudder as the tension I felt dropped away.

"Can I ask what you got up to yesterday?" she asked. "You were both sent home to rest, were you not?"

"We were." Was this going to be easier than I expected? "I spent the day watching TV with my wife."

"I should like to meet her one day. How are you feeling now? Do you have any residual effects from the smoke?" This was good. I didn't know Tanya at all and never would. Her kind enquiries were probably nothing more than politeness, but what I took from her demeanour was that she had no clue Ashley was investigating me.

"I feel fine," I replied, which was true unless one took into account my racing heart rate, diabolical anxiety, stomach cramps ... "But listen, Ashley doesn't seem himself today. He's got one arm in a cast, he's limping still, I don't think he's fully recovered from the fire, and I get the impression that while I was resting yesterday, he was working. I don't want to cause the poor guy trouble at home, but I'm worried about his physical and mental wellbeing."

Tanya tutted, a disappointed sound that told me we were on the same page. "Thank you for calling, Tony. I won't let him know that you did, but I will lean on him to slow down. He needs to at least give himself time to recover."

She was intuitive enough to know it would cause friction at work if Ashley knew I'd called her. She was probably thinking up ways to gently force him to think taking it easy was his idea.

That's what Mary would do and only days afterward would I realise I'd been duped.

Now that we had some rapport, I posed the question I wanted to ask.

"Can I ask what he was working on yesterday? We don't have a live case at the moment, and it might help me to know what's going on in his head."

"Sorry, he never really discusses his cases with me, but I can tell you that he had a visitor."

"Really?"

"Yes. A retired cop. Someone called Bryan."

My heart thumped in my chest again.

"I think it was something to do with an old case in Herne Bay. I'm afraid I don't remember anything else he might have said about it, but it had something to do with that old piece of video they were showing on the TV last week. The one with the blonde woman."

Bryan had identified Mary! That had to be it. We never hung out socially back then, but there were gatherings for drinks every now and then, so he knew who she was and what she looked like. I thought Ashley just talked on the phone, but Bryan was invested enough in proving he been right about Bruce being murdered by a cop that he came to meet Ashley in person.

If I hadn't already been sagging against the wall …

"Tony? Are you still there?"

"Yes. Sorry," I mumbled. I was sunk. That was the noose going around my neck. It explained why Ashley asked about why I thought she would be recognised. He knew why. He knew I could tell who it was without looking.

Because I had always known.

I had to end the call but couldn't seem to make my limbs work. My legs felt so weak I wondered if they would give out if I tried to move. In my hand my phone began to vibrate. There was an incoming call. I didn't recognise the number, but it prompted me to put my brain back into gear.

"Sorry, Tanya," I just about managed to articulate a sentence. "I have another call. I'll do my best to keep him out of trouble today." She was going to say something else, but I cut her off before she could. It wasn't like I had to worry about whether she liked me; I was planning to kill her fiancé.

A fantasy image of Mary on the promenade of a beach somewhere in Italy filled my head. Could we escape and live the rest of our lives in peace?

The phone vibrated again and stopped. I had waited too long to connect the call. Racked with indecision about what my next move ought to be, I tapped the number to call it back and with a shaky arm, held the phone up to my face.

Chapter 36

ASHLEY'S EYES WERE GLUED to his screen. The more he thought about it, the more possible it seemed that the blonde woman in the video was Mary Heaton. Bruce Denton was a good-looking man who clearly liked to bed as many women as possible. A chap like that would score a few married ladies along the way and probably not care one jot that he did.

But was it Tony's wife or not? A few of the clues aligned to make it seem likely, but he needed to find a photograph of her from that time. Preferably one with her wearing the same outfit. In a court room the video evidence would be argued by both sides. The quality still wasn't great even after the tech boys did their best to improve it, so even if he found a picture with her wearing the exact same clothes and hairstyle, it wouldn't serve as definitive proof. However, for the purposes of determining the identity of the killer, convincing *himself* he was right was a big step.

For the last half an hour, he'd trawled social media. Tony didn't have accounts on any of the platforms, but Mary did. And there were photographs.

He clicked and scanned, clicked and scanned, looking for an album that might contain pictures from thirty years ago. Of course, back then social media was a concept yet to be imagined and not many people go through the laborious process of getting their old physical photographs converted into digital. Ashley hadn't. The pictures from his childhood would sit in albums on a shelf in his parent's house until they died. He might then inherit them, but doubted he would find the time, effort, or even desire to upload them as digital files.

Consequently, what he wanted to see wasn't there. Accepting defeat, he attempted to work around the problem.

Chapter 37

"THIS IS DETECTIVE SERGEANT Heaton. I have a missed call from this number." I had no idea who was going to be at the other end of the line and wasn't even thinking about it. My mind was elsewhere until the person spoke.

"Oh, hi. I'm glad you called back. This is Leigh at Boots."

In a dark recess of my brain, a small flame sparked into life. I knew the name but needed a moment to recall why.

"The deputy manager?" she prompted me. "You came in with a photograph yesterday."

Ding, ding, ding.

"Oh, yes. Were you able to find out who paid to have them printed?" I assumed that was what she was calling about, but I wasn't about to waste my time trying to solve an old case. For all I knew Ashley already had all the evidence he would need to arrest me. He would show it to my boss and have other officers confirm they agreed with his conclusions before they moved, but it could be happening right now.

"Well, no," Leigh replied, making me wonder why she had chosen to call. "I still have to check where we stand on GDPR, and I don't have a name yet anyway. What I do have is the rest of the photographs."

Had I heard her correctly?

"The rest of the photographs?"

"That's right. There are twenty-two of them. Twenty-three if you count the one you already showed me."

A handful of seconds ago, I was thinking about running. I could be at the port with Mary in a little less than an hour. We would be out of the country in under two hours. But what if I didn't have to run?

It was a long shot, but there was no record of the other photographs in the case file. Maybe they would show nothing, but what if they did? It could provide me the opportunity I needed. If one of the photographs showed that the person wearing Elroy's clothes really wasn't him, we would have instant justification to arrest him. His alibi would simply evaporate. Combined with Rachael Weaver's letter, we would have enough to convince the CPS to move forward. I was sure of it.

That wasn't the point though. I no longer gave a stuff about Elroy Stewart or Daniel Mahony. The point was that Elroy was suspected of violent crimes. In the process of arresting him, my partner would be tragically and very fatally wounded. Weirdly, I no longer felt sick when I thought about it. Suddenly I had a plan, and it was one that could work.

"Leigh, thank you for calling," I replied, holding up my free arm to confirm the shakes had gone. "Please keep those pictures somewhere safe, I'm on my way to you now."

Ending the call, I tapped my pocket and started back through the Whitstable nick. Everything hinged on what the photographs showed, but I was prepared to bluff my way through if it was necessary. Was I planning to kill my partner? Yes. Would I frame Elroy Stewart for his death? Damned skippy.

Moving quickly, I rounded a corner and had to stop sharply to avoid bumping into the person coming the other way.

"Tony," said Ashley.

"Ashley," I blurted, my heart once again jackrabbiting around my chest.

He stared at me, a million questions etched into his features, none of which made it to his lips. I had questions of my own, and for a moment I felt bad about what I was planning to do. He was a bright kid with a great future. He would rise through the ranks, get married, and have kids. Except he wouldn't because he'd figured out what I'd kept hidden for more than half my life.

But had he?

Not yet it seemed. Not without enough confidence to make a move.

"Were you looking for me?" I enquired.

"No, were you looking for me?"

I wanted to get him to continue with whatever it was he was doing so I could leave. But I couldn't tell him about the photographs. If I did that, he would insist on coming with me and that would be a problem if the photographs were no good.

"No, I was ... just heading to the gents," I thought up a believable lie on the spot.

His eyes narrowed a little, assessing me. What I would give to know what was going on inside his head.

"Oh, there you are," said a new voice. It came from behind Ashley and belonged to Geoff Butters, the duty sergeant in the custody centre. "The chap you brought in is ready to be interviewed. The solicitor just got here."

Ashley looked right into my eyes, but he didn't say anything.

"That's great," I said, not meaning it. "We'll be right along."

"You'll need to come and get him," Geoff growled. "I'm not here to fetch and carry for you."

I didn't care for his surly attitude, but snapping back at him wouldn't achieve anything. It was poor timing, but I was going to have to play along. The interview didn't need to take too long, and chances were that Bobby would give us absolutely nothing.

Chapter 38

Ten minutes later, the tape was running and I was sitting next to Ashley on one of those God-awful plastic chairs the universe seems to reproduce constantly. They appear everywhere as though they multiply at night when no one is watching.

Opposite me, Bobby Lamson had recovered from his race through the back alleyways of Whitstable and had a sneer plastered onto his face. Beside him, a thin man in a cheap suit tried hard to keep a little distance between himself and his appointed client.

I showed Bobby the letter and explained what it was. I then read it, building up to the part where Rachael identified Bobby as one of the men who made sure she withdrew her statement twenty years ago.

"That's all you've got?" he snorted his derision. "A letter from a dead lady?"

After feeling awful for most of the day, I was now in my comfort zone. The man opposite me was trying hard to hide his fear and didn't understand how easy he was to read.

"No, Bobby," I replied, leaning forward across the table to spear him with my eyes and make sure he saw how confident I looked, "it's not all we've got." I took the photograph out of the folder and placed it on the table. For the purposes of the recording I explained what we were looking at. "This is a fake," I said, "and we can prove it."

"You're bluffing," Bobby sneered, trying to sound as though I amused him, but yet again he chose the wrong answer. He needed to say that we couldn't because it wasn't a fake, instead he challenged me because it is.

"Am I, Bobby?" I so desperately wanted to tell him about the other photos. I wanted to watch the confidence drain out of his face, but I didn't dare. I had to keep them a secret until I could use them to lure Ashley. It shocked me how calm I felt about my plan to kill him.

I was going to ask Bobby whether he was worried Rachael's daughter would recognise him, but Ashley jumped in with a question of his own.

"Why did you run, Bobby?"

"Couldn't be bothered with the hassle, could I? You pigs are always accusing me of something. I ran because I wanted a peaceful afternoon."

Ashley continued unphased, "The Crown Prosecution Service will consider the letter sufficient to pursue charges against you, Bobby. You will do time, but your bigger concern should be your part in the murder of Daniel Mahony."

"Didn't have nothing to do with it."

"That's a double negative," I pointed out.

Bobby turned his head my way, confusion ruling his face.

I tapped the photograph again. "You're in this picture, Bobby. You gave a statement in 2003 in which you claimed Elroy Stewart was with you."

"Because he was."

I shook my head slowly from side to side. "No, he wasn't. The truth will out, Bobby. Evidence is finding its way into the light. Elroy is going to go down for the murder of Daniel Mahony, but you don't have to do hard time alongside him. You can get ahead of this."

"Yeah? By finally telling you the truth?"

Again he said the wrong thing.

"So there is a truth to reveal," said Ashley.

"That's not what I meant."

"But it is what you said."

Years of interviewing people has given me a sense of whether they will break or not. Most people do if you push them hard enough. Not because the police employ tactics that force them to admit guilt even when they are innocent, but because for most people, once they are trapped in an interview room, they come to accept that they are already caught. It's a relief to finally admit the truth and have it out in the open.

However, there is a subset of the population to whom this doesn't apply. Most people commit their crimes without thinking. Whether acting out of passion in the heat of the moment, or just from being foolishly opportunistic, they never have what one might like to call 'a plan'. In contrast, Bobby, Elroy, and people like them expect to get caught one day. For all I know they practice getting interviewed so they are ready for when it happens.

We could keep going at Bobby for hours and he wouldn't cave. The letter probably wasn't enough to put a case together, but if we could bring down Elroy it wouldn't matter. Bobby's part in perverting the course of justice would become just another element in the murder trial.

A triple murder trial.

Elroy would find himself accused of not only killing Daniel Mahony in 2003, and Emily Harris just yesterday, but also of murdering Detective Sergeant Ashley Long when he tried to place him under arrest. There were a bunch of moving parts I couldn't yet predict, but I could see no option other than to move forward. It didn't serve me to prolong the interview, so I turned my attention to Ashley and dipped my head toward the door – I wanted to speak to him outside.

We paused the tape and stepped into the corridor.

"You were pushing it with the photograph, Tony. We have no way to prove that thing is a fake."

I rather hoped he was wrong about that, but I offered no comment other than to say, "I wanted to see how he would react. The case is opening up. I can feel it." It was hard not to focus on what I believed was going through Ashley's head. I doubted very much that he was focused on Bobby Lamson and his crimes. But what was his next move? Where would he look, who would he talk to in his quest to prove I killed Bruce Denton?

"Not with him it isn't. But I think it's worth approaching the CPS with the letter."

We both knew we would stand more chance if we had something else, but it was worth a try.

"He assaulted a police officer today, so we can charge him with that, but either way we can keep him while we wait for an answer." I didn't care whether we let him go or not, but I maintained the pretence.

"I'll make the call," Ashley offered.

That worked for me. I had been heading to meet Leigh at the Boots in Herne Bay forty-five minutes ago. The day was ticking away, and I couldn't afford to waste time. If the shops closed and I missed my chance ... well, I wasn't sure I would get another. If Ashley was on my trail, tomorrow just might be too late.

Bobby's duty solicitor argued for him to be released, but he did so half-heartedly because he knew it wasn't going to happen. I had to hang around until a constable came to escort Bobby back to his cell, but finally I was free to go.

Keys in hand, I headed for the exit and my car outside. And there I froze.

Ashley was outside and getting into a car. It wasn't his. That was parked at the nick in Herne Bay. Instead it was an unmarked police car. He was going somewhere without telling me.

Chapter 39

ASHLEY PUT THE CAR into gear and winced just a little when he released the clutch. The seat wasn't set up right, so he adjusted it, lowering the base so the action of moving his leg didn't impact his hip so much.

Pulling out into the lazy November traffic, he ran through his plan once more. He could have kept going on social media, looking for someone who had old pictures of Mary Heaton, but he wasn't confident he would find what he needed no matter how many hours he afforded the task. But there was a place where he thought he might find what he needed.

And he was going there right now.

Mary would be surprised to see her husband's partner on her doorstep, but he had a ruse figured out in his head. Tony was due to retire in less than two weeks. There would be a gathering at the Herne Bay nick and a speech by the superintendent. The guys would have had a whip round to get him a gift that Tony, like most recipients of such things, would shove in a drawer and never think about again. There would be drinks at some local boozer with Tony getting his pocket lightened to the tune of a round for everyone who showed up and that would be that. As his partner for the last month and probably almost right up until his last day, Ashley would be invited.

With that in mind, his visit to Mary would be under the pretence that he wanted to plan something bigger and better. If he was right about it all, she was the woman in the video, but would she know he was there because of that? Tony suspected he was onto him, that much was obvious, and the fact that he hadn't confronted Ashley to ask why he was acting differently made his possible guilt seem all the more likely.

Ashley hated that it could be true. He would have to arrest the man who saved his life. Fervently, he prayed he was wrong, but he didn't think he was. Had that been the case, he wouldn't be on his way to find evidence at his partner's house. A strand of hair, that would do it. It would be proof. Or not.

The forensic guys could turn a DNA sample around in hours if they were pushed (or motivated) to do so. If Mary's hair matched that taken from Bruce's pillow thirty years ago ... well, it couldn't really get more definitive than that. Even so, a strand of her blonde hair wasn't all he wanted. A picture of her from around the time the video was shot was right at the top of his list.

He'd never been inside their house, and that was going to make finding what he wanted far harder. Especially with Mary in the house.

Unless she was out.

If no one answered the door, it would present him with a new conundrum. Breaking in would make the evidence inadmissible but also made it far more likely he would find it. Tossing a house doesn't take long if you know what you are doing.

Unable to guess whether Tony's wife would be home or not, he parked the car at the end of the drive and stepped out onto the pavement. Loaded with ulterior motive, he set his expression to amicable and enthusiastic before setting off down the sloping garden path to the house.

There was no sign of life; no sound from a music system or television, nor movement visible through the window, but when he knocked on the door, he saw a shape move in the distance. The frosted glass made it indistinct, but Ashley could tell it was Tony's wife. Not that he expected it to be anyone else.

Hoping he wouldn't now discover she had a friend or friends around, he waited for her to answer the door.

Chapter 40

I WATCHED HIM PARK and walk to my house. He vanished from sight, and I had to move forward to continue watching.

What was he doing? Was he going to arrest Mary? The possibility had never occurred to me, but if Bryan Hayworth had identified my wife as the woman in the video, was it so surprising that he would take her into custody? She hadn't come forward despite the video being all over the local news and social media feeds, and even though he wouldn't suspect her of the murder, the fact that she was my wife and hiding the fact that she knew the victim made her actions highly suspicious.

I gripped my steering wheel so hard it made my hands hurt. I could burst in on them right now, but that would put all the cards on the table. What if he was just here to ask a few questions? Mary was no slouch. She wouldn't give anything away.

When she opened the door, their exchange looked pleasant. Certainly, he didn't pull out a set of cuffs and pin her against a wall. Mary stepped back while beckoning that he follow. Why would she do that? I lost sight of them both when she closed the door.

Grinding my teeth, I got out of my car and edged up to the hedge bordering my neighbour's front lawn. It would do me no good to have Ashley spot me, but I had to know what was going on.

Taking out my phone, I paused. If I called her, he might hear that it was me. He thought I was back at the nick in Whitstable. In fact, he probably thought I was wondering where he was and hoping I hadn't noticed that he'd snuck away. I couldn't call but I could text. So that was what I did.

'Mary, don't let Ashley know I am texting you. I just followed him here. What does he want?'

Fretting, and praying my neighbours didn't come out to see what I was doing hiding behind their hedge, I waited for my wife to reply. Glaciers melted, tectonic plates collided, and finally the little ellipsis thingy appeared to show me she was typing.

'He says he wants to organise a special retirement party for you, not the usual drinks at the pub that everyone else gets.'

I sucked in a hard breath and typed, '*Don't believe a word of it. He's onto us. I have a plan and it's going to work. Just be polite, don't tell him anything, and if he asks about the video, lie through your teeth.*'

I got back, '*Okay xx.*' Which made me feel bad because we always put kisses at the end of our messages and I had forgotten. Thinking she would forgive me given the circumstances, I gave myself a moment to think.

With Ashley in my house, I at least knew where he was even if I didn't exactly know what he was doing. The sun was already dipping toward the horizon, and the shops would shut in a little more than an hour. That gave me enough time to get to Boots to collect the photographs Leigh had for me, and it had to be my priority task. They were my bait. They would bring Ashley to me.

Chapter 41

"THANK YOU, MARY. TEA would be lovely." Ashley smiled and watched her open a cupboard. She took out two matching mugs and closed the door. She was nervous, that much was obvious from her movements. She almost dropped one of the mugs as she tried to set it on the counter.

"Butterfingers," she blushed.

The text message from Tony had come through just as she came into the kitchen. Her phone was on the counter, the screen facing the ceiling so if Ashley got close enough he would not only see who it was from but be able to read the message.

Mary was surprised to find Ashley on her doorstep, and equally so when Tony revealed he was following him. It made her gut tighten. Positioning herself so the phone was impossible to see, she didn't answer it straight away. She had a guest, so paying attention to her phone would be rude. But she had seen who the text was from and needed to read it properly.

While the kettle boiled, and Ashley explained why he was there without Tony, she tapped the phone screen and had to fight not to react when she read the replies. Tony had already told her Ashley was getting too close to the truth, and now he made it sound like they were about to be caught.

The bags were next to the sofa in the living room. She was ready to go, just like he instructed.

But Tony said he had a plan. Mary could only imagine what that might entail, but she didn't like it. He'd already raised the possibility that he might have to kill his partner, but Mary wasn't so sure he had it in him. Killing Bruce Denton was different. Had he told her in advance that he was going to do it, she would have talked him out of it. That's why he kept it secret and pretended to be working a case that night. Only afterward did he reveal the truth. The memory of them holding each other flooded back, huddled on the kitchen floor while he assured her he would never be caught.

That her husband was a killer had never bothered her. In many ways it made her feel safer, but this was not the same. It wasn't even close. Tony was a gentle man, even if he didn't like to admit it.

Putting the phone down and handing Ashley his steaming mug of tea, she asked, "What do you need from me?" If this was a ruse, he was going through with it, and she had to play along.

"Well, I have a few things organised, but one thing I want to do is mark the passage of time. This is a celebration of a person who has given their working life to the service of the community. I'm sure you must have photographs of Tony when he was younger. His passing out picture from the academy? One of him in uniform? Anything that shows his time as a police officer will do."

Ashley wanted to get his hands on their photograph albums. That was the aim. There had to be pictures of Mary that showed what she looked like thirty years ago. All he had to do was get his hands on them.

Taking a sip of his tea, which was far too hot still, Ashley said, "I don't want to take up too much of your time, so if you're okay with it, I can take them away and go through them tonight. I promise I'll bring them back tomorrow."

Mary didn't like that plan but felt nervous about turning him down flat. Instead, she said, "How about if we look at them now? I haven't had the old photo albums out in years. If you see anything that suits your needs, you can take them to be copied."

Ashley nodded with a smile. It wasn't what he hoped for, but so long as he got to look through them … He expected that Mary would be more suspicious, but she left the kitchen only to return a few moments later with a hefty stack of old, faded albums in her arms. She was gone for less than a minute, but that was more than enough time for him to scour the floor and worktops for a few strands of her hair.

He found two long ones on the back of a kitchen stool. They all went into an evidence bag which was securely in his pocket by the time his host returned.

Stepping back so she could deposit the albums on the counter-top, he counted five. They didn't match. They weren't even the same size, but that was just what he would find in his parents' house and were the situation not so grave, it might have made him smile to think of all the memories locked inside.

Picking one from the pile, Mary said, "I haven't looked at these in years, but I think they cover the early part of his career." She flipped it open to the first page, discovered she had it back to front and flipped it over. "No," she decided in less than a second.

She grabbed the next one and repeated the process.

Ashley took the album she had discarded. "May I?"

Mary didn't look up, but said, "Sure." She didn't know what else to do. If Tony said Ashley was lying about his reason for being there and he really was onto them, how was she supposed to play it? If his interest in obtaining old pictures of Tony was real, this is how she would act. She wanted to kick him out, but what would that achieve? Maybe if she kept him around and got him talking he would reveal something that would help them.

She just didn't know and trying to figure out what to do ate up all her brain power.

Chapter 42

THE SUN WAS ALMOST fully down by the time I parked my car and walked through town. Lights from inside the shops illuminated the street and there were people around doing their shopping. I passed a Christmas display and a sign advertising an imminent toy event where shoppers could enjoy three for the price of two on a range of products.

My days of buying toys were far behind me, but I couldn't help but question what Christmas would be like for me this year. Would I spend it with Mary and our daughter as we usually did? Or would I be in jail or on the run?

It would be decided today. Almost certainly in the next few hours. I quickened my pace, wanting to be done with the tension that wanted to crush me with its crippling grip.

I pushed through the door to get into the small Boots pharmacy and went straight to the first member of staff I could see.

"I'm looking for Leigh Sage," I announced, showing them my warrant card. "She has something for me," I added so they wouldn't see a need to get excited and speculate what she had done.

The young Asian woman I was talking to had the name Deepna on her badge. She said, "I think she's in the back. I'll take you through."

There was only one customer in the shop, a man in his forties who held two packs of nappies, one in each hand. Walking by I could see they were different sizes.

"Buy both" I advised. "You can always bring the wrong ones back."

He didn't answer, but looked my way as I passed by. When I reached the door to enter the 'staff only' area, he was walking toward the till with both packs in his basket.

Leigh was in the same windowless, featureless office she took me to the first time I met her. Facing a wall, her eyes were on the screen to her front.

Deepna stuck her head through the office door. "There's a police officer to see you, Leigh." She was short at five feet two or three inches so when Leigh swivelled her chair around to look, she clocked me looking over the top of the Asian woman's head.

Deepna wasn't interested enough in our business to hang around, leaving us to return to the shopfloor the moment she had delivered me.

"I got caught up with a suspect," I said, explaining why it had taken the best part of two hours to get to her when I said I was leaving immediately.

Leigh reached down to open the filing cabinet that formed one leg of her desk. It needed a key to unlock the mechanism though I knew it wasn't the kind of lock that could keep a person out if they had even the slightest determination to see inside.

"I was starting to wonder if you were coming." Pulling the drawer open all the way, she leaned over to pluck a white package from behind the drop files. "I put it in here for safe keeping."

My fingers itched with the need to see the pictures. I could make my plan work if they were all useless, I would just have to lie harder, but if there was one that showed me something ...

Leigh handed me the package which turned out to be nothing more than a padded A6 envelope. The photographs, all six inches by four, were inside. I tipped them carefully into my hand.

My heart fluttered. The first picture and the next and the next were all of the same group on the same night. Bobby Lamson was there, so too Helen Hoath-Salter. I could identify the other individuals but leafing through I was only interested in one person: Elroy Stewart.

Or whoever it was wearing his clothes.

In the picture that secured his alibi and prevented the CPS from pursuing a conviction the first time, the Elroy character was caught in semi-profile. He was sitting on the boot of a convertible BMW M3, facing to the right and touching his face. The clothes he wore were confirmed as Elroy's and his lawyers had provided other photographs taken at different times with Elroy wearing the same outfit.

I worked through the deck, scrutinising each picture for a few seconds before moving it to the back of the pack. Leigh said there were twenty-two photographs. I hadn't counted but I had to be about all the way through them when I found it.

Leigh had remained in her office chair, silently watching me, but I guess she saw my expression change because she stood up and came to stand beside me, craning her neck a little to get a better look.

The pictures were all taken on the same night and all within a period that lasted less than five minutes. They were staged, that much was clear, and they had picked one that provided enough ambiguity that no one could easily challenge the claim that Elroy wasn't in fact ... um, Elroy.

Quite why no one from the original team of investigators thought to check if there were other photographs I would never be able to say, but with a smile like the Cheshire Cat spreading across my face, I knew we had him.

In my hands, at the top of the pack of pictures, was a shot that showed the face of the man wearing Elroy's clothes. He had a can of beer in his hand and a wide smile. A smile that didn't contain his gold incisor. In the Daniel Mahony case file were the pictures taken at Whitstable nick when Elroy was arrested and processed. His gold incisor was right there for everyone to see.

I had him.

Breaking another decades old cold case and bringing a killer to justice wasn't at the top of my list of things to do. Heck it wasn't even on the list, but for concealing Ashley's murder and pinning it on Elroy, this was the absolute jackpot. He'd killed before and then intimidated everyone who could possibly ruin his alibi. He would be seen as a very bad man and no one would doubt his guilt when I claimed he was the one who stabbed my partner.

Heck, I was probably going to get a medal, but Elroy would deny the charge, and it would be hard to get his fingerprints and DNA on the weapon.

But I had a plan for that too.

If I wasn't feeling lightheaded and giddy from the adrenalin, I might have managed a smile at how it was all working out.

"I take it you're seeing something helpful," Leigh said, looking up at me. The photograph in my hand meant nothing to her.

I wanted to grab her face and kiss her lips. This was the best gift I could be given. Now all I had to do was enact the final part of the plan. If I pulled this off, when I finally got home tonight and it was all over, I would pour myself a large measure of the best whisky I had. I wanted it now, but my head had to be clear.

With a breath to steady myself, I put the photographs back into the padded envelope.

"Leigh, you have single-handedly bought a killer to justice. When they have a press conference later, is it okay if I give them your name?" I was being generous, of course. Leigh hadn't performed any detective work, but without her efforts, bringing Elroy to justice would have been a tougher proposition.

I had been prepared to lie and then to claim the photograph showing him was destroyed had there not been one that so clearly showed it wasn't really him in the picture. That version would have been trickier, but I had been at the point where desperate plays were all I had left.

Leigh's cheeks coloured. "I didn't really do anything."

"But what you did will make all the difference. Can I use your name?" Anything to distract the press from looking too hard at me.

Looking like she was in two minds, Leigh mulled it over before saying, "I guess."

I thanked her again and meant it. She had come through for me when it would have been easy enough to have done nothing or placed the task at the bottom of the to do list.

Leaving the shop, I pulled my coat tighter around my neck. The temperature had dropped, and I was going to be outside for the next few hours. I had the tools I needed to end it all and come out on top. However, whether I succeeded or not was going to come down to luck. I just had to hope that mine held for a little bit longer.

Chapter 43

ASHLEY CAUGHT HIMSELF STUDYING the pages of the albums more than once, each time resuming a casual demeanour as though this was a fun task and nothing more. His eyes skimmed the images, looking for shots of Mary. All he needed was one that convinced him she really was the woman in the video. Finding her wearing the same clothes was probably too much to hope for, but the hair might be enough.

"How about that one?" asked Mary.

Ashley looked up, meeting her gaze which flicked back down to the album under his nose.

"You just missed one," she said and reached across to turn back the page.

In his haste to find pictures that might confirm his theory about Mary, he'd missed the one that showed Tony holding up his three stripes. In the photograph he looked elated and probably was. Ashley could recall how he felt when his promotion was confirmed. He was self-assured enough to know it was coming. He was better at his job than anyone else vying for advancement and worked harder. Yet having the promotion confirmed still came as a huge relief. It was confirmation that his superiors valued his efforts.

But the picture of Tony was precisely what he told Mary he was looking for, and he'd skipped right by it.

"Goodness, yes," he tried to cover up his error. "How did I miss that?"

"How indeed," said Mary, her tone a little too hard. To cover up how badly she wanted to ask what he was really looking for – it was blindingly obvious it wasn't photographs of her husband, she took the album and began to peel back the cellophane cover. "I'll get that out for you. I will get these back, right?"

"Oh, absolutely. I'll have copies made tomorrow. It might take me a couple of days to get these back to you, though. I spend most of my time with Tony and I need to keep this secret if we want it to be a surprise."

Seeing an opening, Mary asked, "Yes, how come you're not with him now? Where is he?" She lifted the photograph out from under the cellophane and placed it in front of Ashley once she had smoothed the clear plastic sheet down again.

Ashley moved the picture to one side, so it was out of the way and took the album back. The period he was looking at was right around when Bruce was murdered. If he was going to find a picture that showed Mary looking like the woman in the video it was going to happen over the next few pages.

But it didn't.

There were photographs, but none that showed her looking undeniably like the woman who walked down the road with Bruce Denton. Reaching the penultimate page, Ashley accepted that he wasn't going to find what he desired. It didn't mean he was wrong, but he absolutely couldn't move forward until he was unshakeably certain with the kind of evidence that would convince others.

He turned to the final page and was about to flip the album shut when his eyes caught sight of the picture at the top. Mary was in it, but he wasn't looking at her. He was looking at what she was standing next to.

It was a car.

She was posing with the driver's door open like the proud owner of a newly purchased vehicle. Ashley figured that was precisely what it was.

The car itself was unimportant. What mattered was its number plate. It ended with FUN.

Chapter 44

MARY WATCHED ASHLEY LEAVE with an itchy, nervous feeling in her stomach. He'd seen something in one of the pictures. Abruptly, he had announced a need to be somewhere else. He was very apologetic, but he had to go. He'd gathered up the photograph of Tony holding his stripes and two other pictures she had found and he asked her for an envelope or something he could put them in.

She had to leave the kitchen to find one and when she came back the photograph albums were all closed and stacked neatly on the countertop.

The moment he went out the door, she ran back to the kitchen, opened the album he was looking at when his urgent need to be elsewhere arose, and tried to figure out what it was that he saw.

She found it instantly.

Or rather, she didn't.

There was a picture missing from the very back page. He'd taken it, but she hadn't seen what it was. Pursing her lips and wishing she could remember what the photograph might have shown, she noticed a faint outline in the cellophane. It was hard to make out against the dark paper of the page, but placing the spare white envelope she brought through behind the cellophane, she saw it. The picture had been pressed against the cellophane for so long, some of the colours had leached into the plastic to leave a ghostly impression of the image.

It was her car.

Why would Ashley want to steal a picture that showed her and the car? With a gasp, her brain provided the answer. It wasn't the car at all. It was her. She couldn't remember what she was wearing that day, but it had to be the same dress she had on the day she found herself at Bruce's house. It had been burned long ago at Tony's insistence, but she remembered it as clear as any item she had ever worn. It was burned into her memory like a brand.

That had to be it. Ashley saw her in the dress and knew she was the woman in the video. She felt faint. He'd come looking for evidence and she'd given him all he would need to put her husband away for the rest of his life.

Snatching panicked breaths, she ran back through the house to the front door.

Ashley was just pulling away! She wasn't too late.

Still wearing her house slippers and without a coat, she grabbed her car keys and ran out of the house. There was no plan in her head, no clue what she would or could do, but staying at home to fret wasn't an option. Halfway to the car she stopped.

A glance up the road came in time to see Ashley put his indicator on. He was going to turn left and that would take him to Vicker's Road. That meant he had to be heading back to the nick in Herne Bay. Almost certainly.

Split by indecision, and terrified by the thoughts in her head, Mary ran back into the house. There was something she needed to get.

Moments later, and leaving the house unlocked for there was no time to delay, she backed her car off the drive and tore after her husband's partner.

Chapter 45

I DROVE TO THE Waterfront, Elroy's front for his illegal activities, cleverly disguised as a legitimate business. I have a crappy old pair of binoculars in the glove compartment of my car. They have been there for years. One of the eyepieces has been glued back on and is a little wonky because I performed the task after imbibing multiple whiskies, but they did the job well enough. Using them, I watched his place to make sure he was there. It's no good organising a raid if the target is elsewhere.

For all I knew he was at home or out somewhere. The club is considered to be his base of operations but that doesn't mean he's there all the time. I got lucky though. About fifteen minutes after I started to watch the front entrance and its surrounds, he arrived by car. Showing off his status, he had a driver and was in a Mercedes S Class, a car of some refinement.

He exited the rear of the car, using his own hand to open it – he wasn't quite so high up the local food chain that he had someone to open it for him. I watched him go into the club and the car pulled away again, presumably to park somewhere else.

The club was open at this time of the day and likely had some punters inside, playing snooker and getting drinks at the bar, but it was the kind of place that got busy at night. Most especially at the weekends when they had exotic dancers on the stage.

Putting the binoculars down, I huffed out a hard breath and I picked up my phone. I still felt unsteady and nervous, but it was time to put the plan into action.

My first call went to an old pal in Canterbury. Herne Bay and the other nicks along the coast are too small to justify their own firearms unit. If we ever needed that kind of backup, which didn't happen very often, it came from the big nick in Canterbury, and I am fortunate enough to know the guy in charge.

Chief Superintendent Wayne McKee was once a young man who came under my wing. With a career the length of mine there had been a bunch of those, but he was one who had what it took to climb the ranks. Wayne had flaming ginger hair going to grey at the sides. I knew I couldn't get him to deploy a team purely on my say so, but my call was to grease the wheels and let him know I expected a need to arise in the very near future.

The need was genuine. Taking down Elroy and his people was a task Ashley and I would be ill-advised to attempt by ourselves. I couldn't predict what our suspect might do but wasn't going to be surprised if he put up a fight once he thought he was cornered. Would his people be armed? Probably, yes. Hence the desire to have an armed response unit as backup.

Wayne was kind to me. I was overstepping my bounds by a long way and I'm certain anyone else making the call would have got their butt chewed off followed by a report to their boss so another butt chewing could ensue. But they say it's not what you know and today that was proving true.

I explained who we were about to arrest and why before pointing out that I was less than two weeks from retirement and wanted to avoid ending up as a tired cliché by getting killed on the job right before I was set to start drawing my pension. I didn't have to work very hard to make it sound like I was concerned for my safety.

The second call went to Ashley, who answered on the second ring. "Tony? Where are you?"

I could hear the echoey effect and background buzz that always comes when you are talking to a person who is driving. It meant he had already left my house.

That was good and something of a relief. I was on speaker, so Mary wasn't in the back of his car wearing cuffs. She would have heard my voice and responded had that been the case. It didn't mean he hadn't called for uniformed officers to take her away, but I doubted it. He was investigating a fellow cop and would need to be supremely confident to expose what he was doing to the wider police community.

I had to throw off all the negative emotions swirling around my brain, beating them into submission so I could come across as enthused and excited.

"Ashley, you're not going to believe this! I've got the evidence!" I let my cryptic statement sink in for a second. "We can bust Elroy! Right now! Man, you've got to see it. It's solid gold!"

As expected, my outburst confused him. "Hold on. Tony, what are you talking about? What evidence?"

"The photograph, Ashley. We always suspected it was fake, and it is! I tracked down where it was developed ... printed, whatever. It was taken on a digital camera, right?" I took a few moments to explain about the marks on the rear of the photo paper and how I now held all the pictures including one that clearly showed it wasn't Elroy wearing Elroy's clothes.

"It's really that clear?"

I had him. Right under my nose, my partner had been investigating me and while I didn't know how much he had figured out, I was certain he possessed enough evidence to move the case forward. He visited my wife for goodness sake and the only reason to do that was because he knew she was the one who left her hair on the pillow at Bruce's house. He probably had a strand of her hair in an evidence bag right now. If he had the time to get it back to the lab and match it, we were sunk.

"Yes, Ashley. I've tracked him to The Waterfront. He's inside right now. We can have him in a cell before we clock off today." Okay, so arresting a big fish like Elroy Stewart would mean we spent the evening at the nick doing paperwork and conducting interviews to get a confession, but Ashley understood the intended sentiment.

"He's not going to go easy."

I was counting on it.

"I agree. I think we need a firearms unit on standby. If we go in with regular uniforms, there could be casualties." I could practically hear Ashley's brain figuring out the angles. His wins with the last two cases had earned him a degree of infamy. Scoring a third by solving Daniel Mahony's murder would make him look like some kind of supercop, but I was betting my life he was about ready to arrest me. If not now, then soon. That was the score that would identify him as a steely eyed thief taker, and he wanted it so bad he could taste it.

"Okay, I'm coming to you. I'll place the call to Chief Inspector Harris. He'll be able to authorise the firearms unit."

"No, I've got it. I already made the call. They are en route to this location already."

"How did you pull that off?"

"I know Superintendent McKee. I get to call him Wayne."

"And he authorised a unit on your say so?"

"Yup." I was lying through my teeth. My plan required confusion and violence. The more of Elroy's team ended up dead the better. I didn't want any of the cops to get injured, but I was prepared to risk it to save my own neck. "How far away are you? There's no telling how long Elroy might be here."

"About twenty minutes. How far away is the armed response unit?"

This was where it all got tricky. My timing had to be perfect or very close to it.

Chapter 46

ASHLEY LET THE CALL end and stared at the road ahead. He was five minutes from the nick in Herne Bay. The strand of Mary's hair could be in the hands of the forensic guys in no time at all. If it matched the hair found on Bruce Denton's pillow ... but Tony was already in position and ready to bust Elroy Stewart.

He wanted his name on record as the arresting officer.

Yet that wasn't the real drive for turning his car around. Taking the strand of hair to the station for analysis could wait. He wouldn't get an answer immediately, and if it didn't match, it wouldn't change what he knew.

Tony killed Bruce Denton.

Ashley hadn't yet found the time to rerun the VRN check, but when he did, it would reveal a vehicle and a name that wasn't on the version Tony supplied him with. Tony volunteered to run the check so he could doctor it. Vicky's notes never made it in the case file because Tony hid them. It was his car. Or it was Mary's, Ashley conceded, but it made no difference either way whose name was recorded as the legal owner. Finding the photograph of Tony's wife with the car tied all the vague circumstantial evidence together. It no longer felt like he was reaching.

What Ashley didn't know was why his partner chose to kill a seemingly innocent schoolteacher, but there were a few obvious answers. Top of the list was an affair. It was the first thing that occurred to him and still the most likely. Fuelled by rage, Tony murdered his rival. Mary either didn't know, which didn't feel right, or was complicit, which didn't fit. If she was having an affair, why would she keep her husband's murderous secret?

Ashley mused on it while he turned his car around. He had to get to Whitstable as quickly as possible. Hitting the blues and twos, he stomped on the accelerator and swung into the other lane to get around a van.

Was it fear? Did Mary fear her husband might kill her if she ever came forward with the truth? There was nothing about the way they acted as a married couple to make him think that, but he'd seen domestic violence cases before where no one outside of the marriage had any idea it was going on.

Speaking aloud, he said, "If not that, what else could it be, Ashley?"

Forced to slow by an eighteen-wheeler coming the other way, he continued to bully his way through traffic. It was dark and the rush hour was starting to clog the roads. His current route would lead him through the heart of Whitstable, and he'd been driving around the sleepy seaside resort for long enough to know to avoid it at this time of day. Cutting left at the next junction, he took a longer route around the town that would get him to his destination faster.

Deep in his heart, although it saddened him, Ashley knew it didn't matter why Tony chose to kill Bruce. He'd committed murder and had to be brought to justice. The only question was whether he made the arrest the moment he saw him, or after they had Elroy in custody.

Chapter 47

OUTSIDE THE WATERFRONT, I stared at my watch. Ten minutes had elapsed since Ashley gave his ETA of twenty minutes. In average traffic the drive from Canterbury to Whitstable is twenty minutes. But the armed response unit would be coming from the police HQ which was this side of the ancient city. Add to that the speed at which they would be moving, and it was probably more like twelve minutes to get from A to B.

With a nod of my head, I accepted that it was time.

Using my mobile phone because the radio would ensure everyone heard it, I dialled the number for the firearms unit. Not to the boss this time, but to the desk.

When a voice replied less than half a heartbeat later, I dropped my voice to an urgent whisper.

"Officer in trouble. My partner has been stabbed." I gave the address, adding panic to my voice, while simultaneously making it sound like I was fighting to remain professional, I said, "We are trapped inside the building and there are multiple assailants looking for us. I believe they are armed with semi-automatic weapons. I cannot give an accurate headcount but estimate at least five armed suspects. You should enter the property from the front. We cannot get to the doors but might be able to go up to the next floor. Hurry."

The voice of the officer at the other end was calm and encouraging. "Help is on its way. Do what you must to stay alive."

I could only imagine the sudden burst of activity at the other end. "We lost our radios when they attacked and we ran," I reported. "We underestimated their numbers." Then I swore and made out like there was someone coming so I could end the call abruptly.

I was past the point of no return. The team would already have their wheels rolling. If they arrived and nothing was happening, I would be in deep doodoo, but since I believed Ashley was on his way to arrest me, that hardly mattered. I was betting everything on the dice landing exactly where I needed them.

If my heart beat any faster it was going to explode.

Making fists to stop my hands shaking, I gave myself a two-count and called Ashley.

"Hey," I said the moment he answered. My voice was back to a suppressed whisper. "There's something going on here. I can see movement around the back of the club. How far away are you?"

Ashley shot back, "Five minutes."

That was good. He would get to my location ahead of the firearms team. Arriving to find them on site would be a disaster.

I whispered, "I'm moving closer. I need to see what's going on. When you arrive, look for my car. Park next to it and come around to the back of the club. I'll be looking for you."

"Tony, no ..."

I cut him off.

There was nothing happening at the back of the club, but there soon would be. By the time Ashley arrived, just a few minutes ahead of the firearms team, I would be in position. I had to create enough noise to make Elroy send someone to investigate.

I might even start a fire; that always creates panic and confusion.

The firearms team would come in at the front, and I would stab Ashley around the back where no one could see. There would be actual blood on my hands but that was easily explainable by my efforts to save his life.

I even had a knife in the car that I could use, an old fold-out thing with a five-inch blade. It lived in the glove box with the binoculars and some other items that had been in there for so long I couldn't recall how or why they came to be in the car. None of that mattered. It was untraceable. Even I couldn't remember where I bought it.

It was likely that Elroy and friends would be flushed out through the back of the club when the raid started, but I wasn't going to use hope as a strategy. The moment Ashley died, I was going inside to find Elroy. It didn't matter who I framed for Ashley's murder, anyone would do, but I knew I was probably going to have to kill them as well so they couldn't talk. I would be injured in the fight, getting stabbed by the same knife which I was then heroically brave and tough enough to pull from my own body to use on my attacker.

I had it all figured out.

Chapter 48

CHECKING FOR CAMERAS WHILE telling myself Elroy wasn't paranoid enough to have someone inside watching a set of TV screens, I made my way around to the back of the club. Positioned as it was, right on the waterfront, the area behind was open. To access it all a person had to do was go around the far end of a rusty chain link fence.

The yard, if that's the right term for it, had stacks of empty pallets along one side. There had to be a hundred of them at least. An old Ford transit van from the nineties, its front right wheel missing, sat forlornly in the back corner next to a trailer with a RIB on it. A tatty canvas covered the RIB and sitting on top of that was a ginger cat with a ragged ear. It eyeballed me with an indifferent expression. Elsewhere, a trio of dilapidated fruit machines huddled in a row beside a stack of lumber. Out of sight from the public, the back end of the club served as a service yard to store materials that might come in handy and as a place to ditch broken things until someone got around to properly disposing of them.

Making my way through the yard and around the junk, I kept an eye on the road. The firearms team wouldn't use their sirens. They would park out of sight and approach on foot. They would also do whatever they could to establish contact with me. As though my thoughts made it manifest, my phone began to vibrate. My radio was in the car and would find its way into a bin. Having reported it lost, I needed to make that happen.

I didn't need to see the screen to know it was them calling, but I wasn't going to answer. In fact, the best thing for me to do was ignore their calls. They were responding to a distress call and would enter the building looking to rescue two officers in trouble. Their approach in such circumstances would be anything but subtle.

That was exactly what I wanted.

Approaching the rear of the building I had the choice of a steel roller door or a fire door that sat next to it. There were no windows on the ground floor, and that presented a problem. I had no way to know how long I had until Ashley or the armed response unit arrived, but needed to gain access to the building before either of them got here. This really wouldn't work if I was stuck outside.

Imagine my relief when I grabbed the knob and the fire door swung open. It felt like my lucky stars were lining up to approve my plan.

Now all I had to do was find something that would burn. Just a small fire, not like the inferno that almost engulfed me and Ashley two nights ago.

Chapter 49

ASHLEY STOPPED HIS BORROWED car right behind Tony's. He took pride in always being in control of his emotions. In fraught situations, he was the one who demonstrated emotional intelligence. It was why he was going to make it all the way to chief constable, but right now he couldn't figure out what he was supposed to feel. Or think. Or do.

He needed to arrest Tony. Arguably, that was the number one task on his list. But he also needed to support Tony so they could arrest Elroy Stewart. Tony claimed he had evidence that completely changed the case. In his last call, Tony said he saw something and was moving to get a better look. Since then he hadn't answered his phone, and that was worrying.

Ashley tried him again only to get the same result.

If a firearms team was on their way, he could wait for them to arrive. It was the safe play, but if Tony wasn't answering because he'd been hurt, Ashley knew it would make it look as though he was cowering outside when he ought to be at his partner's side.

There was no good answer.

Exiting the car and closing the door quietly, Ashley tried to spot his partner. Tony told him to come around to the back of the club, so that was what he had to do. Moving cautiously, but not so stealthily that anyone seeing him would know he was up to something, he sidled along the rusty chain link fence. Reaching the end he went around and into the yard behind the club.

There was no sign of Tony anywhere, but a door in the rear façade lay open like a taunt. Huffing out a frustrated breath, Ashley checked around, looking for faces in the windows of the second floor. If he was being watched, they were staying out of sight.

At the door, he peered inside. His right foot twitched. Going inside was a legal grey area. He could argue he was conducting a search as part of an ongoing investigation, but he'd been ordered to drop the Daniel Mahony case and wasn't permitted to go anywhere near Elroy Stewart. For the same reason he hadn't called into dispatch to let anyone know where he was going. The moment DCI Harris or Superintendent Charters found out he was disobeying their direct order to stay away …

And it wasn't the first time. Since partnering with Tony he'd stepped over the line more times than he had in the rest of his career added together. DCI Harris had raged at him during the Craig Chowdry investigation. Assuming Tony was right about the new evidence, he could justify his defiance, but what if Tony was wrong?

Was it wrong to be so career minded? Ashley knew it probably was, but there was more at stake here than a reprimand. There were two killers inside the building and only he could ensure they both saw justice. Elroy would get his eventually, even if not today, but so far as Ashley could tell, not one other person on the planet knew Tony Heaton had killed Bruce Denton.

With adrenaline heightening all his senses, Ashley stepped over the threshold and let the door shut behind him.

The door led into a narrow corridor roughly twenty feet long. There were two doors that he could see, one to the left and one to the right, both about ten feet in. Ahead the corridor simply ended, but poor lighting made it hard to see what lay beyond.

Keeping his footsteps light, he used his phone to send a message to Tony. He had no reason to believe it would be answered, but reaching the doors, he spotted his partner. He was inside a large room – the one behind the roller door – and ... what the heck was he doing?

Chapter 50

"TONY?"

I froze. I hadn't heard him approaching and he got here quicker than I expected. He said five minutes and I figured that meant arriving outside.

"What the hell are you doing?" he demanded, crossing the room with a look of furious disbelief on his face.

I considered the question to be rhetorical since I had very obviously just built and lit a fire. The room was multipurpose, and one use was as a place to tinker with cars. I found oils and rags and other flammable liquids in plentiful supply. The fire wouldn't take out the building because it was set away from other materials it could consume, but it would set off the fire alarm (or I would), and it would create a whole load of smoke.

Before I turned around, I reached up with my right hand to touch the hilt of the knife. I had it in my jacket pocket, ready to be employed. I could do this. I had no choice. It was him or me. But I needed him to not only be close, but also paying no attention to what I was doing.

"I'm flushing them out," I replied as if that would explain my actions. I faced him, levelling a serious but grim face. All I had to do was manoeuvre our relative positions. Once he was where I needed him ... "The firearms team will come through the front ..."

"You killed Bruce Denton."

I stopped talking mid-sentence.

Ashley looked surprised. His expression made me think he hadn't planned to blurt the accusation. Beside me the flames took hold. The fire could be extinguished in a moment. There was an extinguisher a few yards away next to the controls for the roller door, but neither of us moved to get it.

My first thought was to laugh and deny it, but there was no point. Ashley wasn't guessing. He knew.

"You doctored the evidence, didn't you? You made sure you got the case so you could control the investigation and then you spent years checking and rechecking with everyone associated with Bruce Denton so you could be sure there were no surprise revelations."

I stared at him, saying nothing. I could do it. I could kill him. I needed to kill him. I just had to get him to come closer. If I pulled the knife he would run. Or knock it from my hand. He might have a limp and an arm in a cast, but his ninja abilities would still outmatch my fighting skills.

"The camcorder wasn't stolen, was it?"

I couldn't get my lips to move.

"You knew Mary would be recognised ..."

"Don't say her name!" I barked.

"Why, Tony? Because she was having an affair and you killed her lover? Has she lived the last thirty years in fear that you might to do the same to her?"

My mouth hung open. The smoke was beginning to fill the air. The room was a large space so most of it was gathering at the ceiling, but it was contained there and I knew it wouldn't be long before I would feel it catching in my throat.

The fire alarm went off, the shrill sound impossible to ignore, but that's what I did.

"Is that what you think?" I had to shout to be heard above the wailing claxon. "You think she was having an affair, and I killed Bruce to get revenge?"

Above us, feet ran across the floor. We heard shouts and barked commands. The firearms team was in the building. I was going to run out of time, but I was going to get the truth off my chest first. It felt like I had waited my entire life to reveal why Bruce had to die. Only Mary knew and nothing could have stopped me from explaining how motivated I was back then.

"He raped her," I spat. It was perhaps the first time I had ever spoken the word while thinking about my wife. "He drugged my wife, and he raped her."

Ashley's expression changed. His hard glare softened, not in sympathy, but with surprise and horror and in question. He wasn't convinced I was being truthful.

A staccato burst of shots rang out. I couldn't tell which side had opened fire, but a gunfight broke out above our heads.

"It was the early nineties, Ashley. Rohypnol was a strange new thing we were just hearing about on the news. In the States, there had been a few cases that went to court, but prosecution and conviction were rare, and the sentences were light. They were laughable."

"So ... what? You took the law into your own hands?"

"Mary wasn't the only one. She was just the last."

Ashley recalled what Angela told him about the women who raged at Bruce in town and how that was the last straw for their relationship.

Stomping feet, the squeal of pain when someone was hit ... this formed the audio backdrop to our conversation.

"Mary came home crying one night. She been out with friends for someone's birthday and there was drinking. I knew something was wrong when she was so late to get home, but she didn't know where she had been. I could tell she was drugged, but thought she had taken whatever it was willingly. I shouted at her, demanding answers. I remember how I hated myself when I figured it out. Her underwear was gone. Bruce kept his victims' knickers as trophies. We didn't have sex for two years, but Bruce was dead within a week."

"How did you find him?"

I couldn't tell if Ashley asked the question to keep me talking, or because he wanted to know the full picture. I was giving him a confession, and, in his shoes, I would also have tried to draw out as much information as possible.

The shooting continued. No more than fifteen seconds had passed since the firearms team stormed the building looking for us. How long would it be until they overwhelmed Elroy and his hoodlums?

The smoke was getting thicker, but the fire itself was almost out. I deliberately gave it only a small amount of material to consume. It was never supposed to burn for long.

I moved my arm so I would feel the outline of the knife though my clothing. I took a step closer to Ashley. When I made my move, I was going to have to be fast.

"Good old detective work. It really wasn't that hard. Mary told me which bar they were in. I spoke to the bar staff, I asked her friends."

"But you didn't talk to any of them when you were investigating his murder."

"Of course not. And neither did anyone else. I was meticulous and careful. Despite that, I was spotted in my car staking out his house."

"Yes, I have a photograph of Mary with the car." Ashley took an envelope from his inner jacket pocket, but didn't bother to take out the picture to show me. "I'm sorry, Tony, but you know how this has to end. You need to give yourself up."

He was asking me to surrender myself.

"He was never going to face justice, Ashley. Even if I could prove he raped Mary. Even if other women came forward. Even if he was convicted, he would be out again in a few months and back to his old ways. I found twenty-three pairs of knickers in his house. They were in a drawer in his bedroom, right next to a supply of rohypnol." They went with me that night and were burned down to ashes which I threw into the sea.

"I get it, Tony. I really do. I can only imagine what I might want to do if someone attacked Tanya, but you broke the law, Tony. You murdered a man. It's not our job to deliver justice."

"I have to disagree. I took an animal off the streets, Ashley. I have never once regretted it."

Ashley looked me dead in the eye. "Will you turn yourself in?"

He was asking if I would come quietly. He believed I was going to go to jail and either I surrendered, or he would take me by force.

The rushing feet above our heads and the barked commands moved. They were elsewhere in the building, the sounds of running feet fading as they went further from our location.

My opportunity was now. I had to take out the knife and kill my partner or spend the rest of my life behind bars. I willed my right arm to move. All I had to do was stab him. It would be over in moments.

But I couldn't do it.

I might have killed but I'm not a killer. When I took Bruce's life, I did it for my wife. It wasn't for the other women he had raped or for his future victims. Mary asked me to see that he met with justice, and I made it happen. It cost me my career, but for the woman I loved it was worth the price.

Sagging, I accepted my fate. I single tear slipped from my left eye and ran down my cheek. I wasn't going to do well in jail.

Chapter 51

ABOVE US, THE FIREARMS team was winning. I could hear their shouts as they cleared rooms and continued through the club. They would find us soon enough. I reported my partner suffering a stab wound and when they revealed that fact, Ashley would see what my plan had been.

That I couldn't go through with it wouldn't make me look a whole lot better.

Ashley walked to the wall where he collected the fire extinguisher. I stood mute and still while he snuffed out what remained of the fire. My brain felt disconnected from my body.

Only when he placed a hand on my shoulder did I react.

"Outside, Tony. Let's go outside. We can wait there. It will be safer for them to find us in the open."

I think I nodded my head, but if I did the gesture barely registered in my brain.

Ashley steered me across the room and out of the door. We turned left along the corridor, heading for the exit.

The firefight had ended, but the officers were still shouting. It sounded like they were still chasing someone.

At the door, I used my right hand to push it open. Ashley was right behind me. In my confused state, finding Mary outside the door didn't register as anything out of the ordinary. But when she gave a maddened scream and stabbed Ashley in the chest, I was instantly brought back to alertness.

Gasping, I twisted to see. Mary had ducked around me, leading with the knife and now stood, her mouth open, her eyes wide as she stared at what she had done.

Ashley staggered back a pace. The knife was buried to the hilt and had to be right through his heart. He lifted his head to look at me, staggered another pace and collapsed.

"Mary," I gasped her name. "Mary, what did you do?"

She grabbed my right arm with both of hers and tried to drag me away.

"I did it for you, Tony! He came to the house. He knew, Tony! He knew! We have to get away!"

My feet moved, my tiny wife using enough force to pull me off balance so I had to follow, but the next time my foot hit the ground I dug it in and stopped us both. Ashley was dying. I was sure of that. He wouldn't get the chance to share my secret and looking down at his unconscious form, a weight lifted from my shoulders.

But what about the call I placed to report his injury? Any moment now we would be found by the officers from the firearms team and my story wouldn't line up.

Running feet pulled my head up. Mary still had hold of my arm, but I yanked it free. She was crying, her voice pitiful when she wailed for me to come with her. I wanted to, but fate had given me another option.

Elroy saw me blocking his exit and came right at me. He was injured and bleeding from his right shoulder. Red stained his shirt. He'd slipped through the team's clutches, making it down the stairs to seek escape through the back of the building. Only I stood in his way, and he fancied his chances.

I suppose I would too if our roles were reversed. I'm an overweight, over the hill, middle-aged man in poor physical condition. Elroy was going to run right through me.

I plucked the knife from Ashley's chest and let Elroy run into it.

Mary screamed and I had to shush her.

Elroy's momentum bowled me to the ground, but I took him with me, keeping the knife between us so his falling weight would drive it deeper than I could with strength alone. His face was inches from mine, his eyes looking right at me, so I got to see when he realised he was going to die.

He pushed himself upright, trying to get away, but succeeded only in getting to his knees.

Operating on pure willpower and instinct, I tore the knife from his chest, the same way I had with Ashley. It was almost done. I had just one final thing to do.

Well, two, I guess.

Turning to Mary, I slapped her face. It was the first time I had ever struck her, and it was going to be the last. She reacted as expected, snapping out of her near-catatonic state to stare at me in shock.

I kissed her.

"Go, darling. Go home and wait for me there. I will be home in a few hours."

"What?"

I gave her a push. "I cannot do this if you are here, darling. Ashley is dead. This piece of trash," I kicked Elroy so he collapsed sideways onto the ground, "stabbed him. That's all anyone will ever know. Go home and wait for me."

When she didn't move, I thought about slapping her face again. I needed her to run, but snarling, "GO!" in her face did the trick. I could hear her sobbing all the way back to her car. It was parked behind Ashley's. I wanted to know how she had found me and what was in her head when she set off from the house with one of our kitchen knives.

Inside my head, a growing list of 'must remember to-do's' got a new item added near the top. The knife, which was still in my hand, would be gathered as evidence. I doubted anyone would come to my house to inspect the knife block, but I was going to have to discard it regardless.

Not in a bog this time.

Catching a trace of what I thought was footsteps on stairs, I clenched my teeth and stabbed the knife deep into my side. The pain was excruciating. Far worse than I was prepared for. I whimpered, unable to fully suppress my need to cry out.

The footsteps were coming my way; two sets at least and they were talking as they came, confirming areas clear as they swept through the lower level of the building.

"Over here," I called, not needing to add pain and fatigue to my voice for it was genuinely there.

Remembering the knife in my jacket at the last second, I threw it, watched it bounce, slide, and finally drop as it went over the edge and into the sea. Then I snatched the white envelope from Ashley's jacket pocket, stuffing it into my own just before two men in tactical gear exited the door, their weapons up and searching for danger.

I was three yards away and on the ground where my blood was beginning to pool. Propped on one elbow as though trying to get up, I pointed at Ashley.

"Check my partner. He's hurt real bad."

One of the officers stayed where he was, weapon up while the other dropped to a knee. With two fingers, he checked Ashley's pulse.

"He's alive."

Chapter 52 – Twelve Days Later

Superintendent Charters stared at me, his lips set in his usual stern expression.

I swallowed hard and waited to hear what he had to say. Everything in my career had boiled down to this. To these last few moments.

Cracking a rarely seen grin, my boss laughed, "And that was when Tony discovered his fly was undone!"

Everyone laughed at the punchline. What's a retirement speech without an amusing anecdote. Not that the story was all that amusing. Most of the laughter was fake, but that's not unusual either.

Superintendent Charters wrapped up his little speech with a few serious words about my dedication to the job and how many years I had given to enforcing the laws of the land. A final reminder that there would be drinks at The Dog and Duck after the shift ended, and it was all done.

He came across to shake my hand and wish me a happy retirement. I couldn't tell whether he meant it or not, but I did believe he was pleased to see me go. In my place, a younger detective sergeant had already started. My absence wouldn't be felt by many for very long.

On the desk beside me was a bouquet of flowers for Mary and a gift-wrapped package for me, plus the obligatory card signed by everyone at the nick. Poignantly, Ashley's name was in it. Doris, who always takes charge of such things, had begun circulating the card before he died.

It happened in the ambulance on the way to the hospital, but they made it clear he was doomed from the moment the knife entered his chest. It pierced his right ventricle and it was a miracle his heart could still beat when the firearms officer checked his pulse.

Naturally, I was questioned at length about the events, but only after I had received surgery for my wound and agreed that I was well enough to be interviewed. I kept the investigating team at bay until I was convinced the story was straight in my head. My concern was that they would question the timeline, but they didn't. I reported Ashley's injury a full fifteen minutes before it occurred, but no one challenged it.

We were both in line for a King's Gallantry Medal. Ashley's would be awarded posthumously. I made it very clear my partner chose to tackle Elroy despite the injuries he'd sustained when he was struck by a hit and run driver less than two weeks earlier. Elroy gained the upper hand and was able to also stab me as he tried to escape. They bought my crazy tale of pulling the knife from my own body which was how I came to be in line for medal.

I'm not saying it made me proud.

Bobby Lamson, still in custody when he heard Elroy was dead, cut a deal and started talking. Elroy was behind Ashley's little accident, and he had picked a car the same as mine to create confusion. The car, it transpired, was supposed to have gone to the crusher, but Bobby was fed up playing third or fourth fiddle to his childhood friend and chose to buy himself some insurance. The car was in a barn out towards Faversham. Elroy's prints and DNA were still on it, and it still wore a set of number plates that matched mine.

Further confessions came as Elroy's boys, all arrested during the raid at The Waterfront or afterwards in the case of those who weren't there that day, elected to point the finger of blame at the top man. They claimed he killed Emily Harris to keep her quiet. She did his bidding because she owed him money. She should have gone to the police. He was also behind the attack on Helen Hoath-Salter, but his boys were guilty too.

The person in 'the' photograph wearing Elroy's clothes turned out to be a cousin. He was interviewed at length but appeared to have no idea he had ever been Elroy's alibi. He'd been loaned the clothes when he visited with his parents for the day. They were sharp threads and almost brand new. For a teenager hoping to score with a girl, that was exciting. But he confirmed it was him in the pictures and that helped to sew everything together. Christine Westbury and Helen Hoath-Salter gave statements freely once the news of Elroy's death became public knowledge. Helen's testimony would prove especially helpful in bringing the remaining members of the gang to justice.

It was someone else's problem to sort out fact from fiction, but I expected each of those associated with Elroy would end up behind bars for a spell.

The clock on the wall said it was almost a quarter to four. The sun was setting outside and there was nothing left to keep me in work.

Except one thing.

On my desk, a cardboard box contained the few personal belongings I had yet to take home. It didn't amount to much and I was sure the box would go on a shelf in the garage and never be looked at again. Next to it sat the Bruce Denton case file. The official one, not the secret one Ashley made a copy of, was waiting for me to take it back to storage.

No one would ever look at it again. Of that I was almost one hundred percent certain. The cold case taskforce was no more. In the wake of Ashley's death and with the other three teams having solidly wasted more than a month to turn up the square root of absolutely nothing, the Chief Constable for Kent decided it was time to call it a day. The officers involved were reassigned or sent back to their regular jobs in the case of the local liaison chaps like me. When the file on my desk went back into storage, it would be there forever.

Somewhere out there was the copy Ashley made of my secret file. I figured it was probably collected from the house he shared with Tanya by the team writing the report on his death. They hadn't asked me about it, and since a single glance would show it had nothing to do with Elroy Stewart and the case that got him killed, it probably got shoved in a box never to be looked at again.

I attended Ashley's funeral, marching behind his coffin alongside hundreds of other officers. Police dying on active duty is rare enough that the top brass made a big thing out of it, not least because his father and uncles all occupy senior posts. There was TV and newspaper coverage. Two reporters tried to get interviews with me, but I politely refused.

Did I feel bad about Ashley's death? Yes, very much so. Yet, I had to admit I was deeply relieved at the same time. After all, I didn't kill him. Mary and I had talked about it only once. It happened after they released me from hospital.

At home, with some medicinal whisky in my bloodstream despite the doctor's warnings, I asked her what happened when Ashley came to the house. What she told me was much as I expected, but if you asked me if my wife would ever follow a person's car intending to kill them so a secret would remain unspoken, I would have scoffed and laughed.

Yet that's what Mary did.

I guess she was operating on autopilot. Not really thinking about how she would pull it off, she grabbed a knife, jumped into her car, and tracked him. When he turned his car around to head for Whitstable, she thought he'd seen her, but he hadn't. Quite how she managed to stay hidden I would never know, but my guess is that Ashley was just too distracted. He'd discovered I was Bruce's killer and that must have messed with his head.

There was no date yet for the medal ceremony, not that I deserved the stupid thing. But I would attend and smile and let them pin it to me and never think about it again. Mary and I were going on a cruise. Whether it was the right thing to do or not, I had decided the escape money we had hidden away could be put to better use. I wanted to use the time to underline that we were free and clear now. I knew I would never truly believe it, not until I was lying on my death bed, but with time the constant need to look over my shoulder would diminish. Maybe we would move. It would be nice to have fewer geographic reminders.

Picking up the folder, I placed it on top of the cardboard box of belongings and headed down to the archive room. The folder would find its way to central storage where it would join all the other items associated with the Bruce Denton murder inquiry.

By the time I got to my car, I was whistling.

Epilogue – Five Months After Retirement

THEY APPROACHED ME ON a Tuesday afternoon. I was walking the dog. Yes, I have a dog now. His name is Sprocket, and he is a labrador. He's still a puppy but he's growing fast.

I was at the park when they came to me; two men in dark suits beneath darker coats. They were both older than me. One had white hair going thin all over. I figured he had to be in his seventies. The other was a little younger but still a good decade older than me. He looked vaguely familiar. His head was completely bald, a shadow of stubble showing where the last stubborn ring of hair had been shaved away.

"Tony Heaton," the older man addressed me. It wasn't a question, he knew who I was.

I raised my eyebrows and looked at them again. They were police officers. Rather, they had been police officers for like me they were both too old to still be serving. You might ask how I could tell just be looking but trust me, the signs are always there.

"Can I help you?" I asked, reeling in Sprocket who strained to get to the new people who might have treats or want to make a fuss of him.

"Yes, said the older man. I rather think that you can. And, as it happens, I believe that we can help you."

I got a tingling at the back of my head, kind of like when Spiderman knows something bad is about to happen. This wasn't a chance meeting.

"My name is Walter Pipcock," he continued. "My colleague is Dean Tibbet. We are two members of a team who don't officially exist. We want to offer you a job."

"Not interested," I shot back and started walking again.

As I passed them, Dean said, "We specialise in investigating cold cases. Ones like Bruce Denton."

Hearing the name was like ice water going down my spine. I stopped walking and faced them.

"What do you want?" This time my voice came out as a growl.

"Precisely what I said," Mr Heaton, said the older man. "To offer you a job. Our department was formed a very long time ago when it was determined that letting experienced and talented investigators fade into retirement was a wasted opportunity. Each member of the team is handpicked and that is why we are here today to talk to you."

"Still not interested," I replied, hoping they would take the hint. My heart hadn't beat this hard since Mary got adventurous in the bedroom on our cruise and had me do it standing up.

"I think perhaps you should reconsider," said Mr Tibbet. "We have our cases assigned to us and rarely freelance with ones that might take our interest."

The veiled threat wasn't lost on me, but just in case, Mr Pipcock drove the point home.

"If you wanted to, working with us, you could have another look at Bruce Denton's murder. That case plagued you for years, did it not?"

"And weren't you looking into it again when that young partner of yours was killed?" asked Mr Tibbet.

Internally, I sighed. I had foolishly believed it was all behind me.

"A job you say?"

"Yes," Mr Pipcock brightened. "One where you will investigate cold cases and help us bring justice."

"But we don't have to reopen the Bruce Denton case?" I needed to clarify that point.

Both men shook their heads.

"Oh, no," said Mr Tibbet. "Our cases are handed to us, like I said. We operate alongside the regular police officers and detectives, but we have a separate budget."

"Perhaps you would like to meet again on Monday. We can tell you all about it," added Mr Pipcock.

Inside my head, I quietly cursed.

The End

Author Notes:

Thank you as always for reading to the end of the book and beyond. Unless you chose to start here, in which case, please go to the front of the book like a normal person.

As I write these final notes, it is a cool Monday at the start of October in 2025. My desk faces out over my garden and if I take a moment to look up I can see blue tits, sparrows, and robins pecking at seeds and nuts on the feeders hanging from the cherry tree outside. The sun is shining, and in a few minutes, when I have finished writing these author notes, I will take my trio of dachshunds for a walk across the nearby vineyards.

The story about the cop who killed a man and ruined his career to keep his secret occurred to me back in 2019. It originally came into existence as a short story which I wrote for a competition. Honestly, I thought I would win, which of course I didn't. I wasn't even shortlisted.

Regardless, the story stuck with me, begging to be expanded into something bigger and more considered. It took me a while to get there, and it was an enquiry from a literary agent that inspired me to pick it up again. As pretty much always happens with literary agents, I got messed around for long enough that I published the first book myself. Now the original concept of a trilogy is complete and I question whether I should just keep going.

The epilogue sets this up nicely, but I am yet to decide whether I will develop Tony's story or not.

In this book I talk about Ashley's injury and the bruise inside his right hip joint. This came from my personal list of medical maladies. I had it in my head that it would be cool to become an Olympian. Unfortunately, despite being identified as an athletic at a very young age, I was never quite good enough at anything to make the topflight. Tackling various sports as I chased that dream, I tried Luge, the feet-first ice sport for maniacs and people who like to dice with death.

In 2008, I crashed on the run at Winterberg in Germany, slamming onto the ice hard enough to bruise the inside of my right hip. I struggled to walk for weeks. I was clocked doing over 100kph coming out of the previous turn. I chose to quit the sport at that point.

The first recorded use of date rape drugs, specifically Rohypnol, in the context of sexual assault, was reported in the mid- 1990s. Rohypnol, along with other substances like GHB and ketamine, became known for their incapacitating effects, making victims vulnerable to sexual assault. I needed Tony to have a reason for his actions that readers would understand and possibly empathise with. I toyed with many ideas, but this was the one that stuck.

My attention will shortly turn to my most popular series, which is about another retired police officer and his dog. First, I have a vacation with my gorgeous wife and wonderful children. I'm one of those lucky guys who looks at his wife and marvels every day at just how lovely she is. Not just physically, but in a way that complements what I bring to the party. Together, I believe we are a great team, and I cannot imagine life without her. I consider it a privilege to be able to look forward to growing old by her side.

Knowing me as well as she does, Gemma observed that I was struggling to write this book and she was not wrong. Stories come easy to me, the words flowing from my brain and onto the page in an uninterrupted stream. Often, I get more than ten thousand words in a day. But not with this book.

Perhaps it is to do with genre. I write cozy mystery and urban fantasy, both of which I can make up on the spot and which require little to no research. Writing police procedural crime is different. It's more complicated and I must stick as close to reality as I can. I'm not sure how far I stretched things in this book, but I'm aware I was pushing the bounds of what could happen.

It will be some time before I try anything like this again, but I do have other ideas outside of my usual genres.

With the school break over the summer, days out, vacations, my books going into global bookshops, a consultancy role I took on, and a host of other distractions, I have been writing this story since July. That might not seem like very long to some, but I generally write a book a month at least. I hope to get back to that now.

I think that's about all for this set of notes. I need to walk the dogs and clear my brain.

Take care.

Steve Higgs

Free Books and More

Want to see what else I have written? Go to my website.

https://stevehiggsbooks.com/

Or sign up to my newsletter where you will get sneak peaks, exclusive giveaways, behind the scenes content, and more. Plus, you'll be notified of Fan Pricing events when they occur and get exclusive offers from other authors because all UF writers are automatically friends.

https://stevehiggsbooks.com/newsletter/

Prefer social media? Join my thriving Facebook community.

Want to join the inner circle where you can keep up to date with everything? This is a free group on Facebook where you can hang out with likeminded individuals and enjoy discussing my books. There is cake too (but only if you bring it).

https://www.facebook.com/groups/1151907108277718

Printed in Dunstable, United Kingdom